"We need a new plan."

"The plan is fine," Spence snapped. "It was fine—until you had to start making changes. I shouldn't even be here! I'm not a goddamn field agent!"

Bolan didn't waste his breath arguing. The sun was starting to rise. Once they lost the dark, they'd lose the only real protection they had. The militants would realize they were facing only two men, and they'd swarm. Bolan and Spence had to take the fight to the enemy.

Bolan popped a smoke canister out of his harness and pulled the pin. He lobbed the grenade over the wall and immediately grabbed another. "Get ready to move," he said as he sent the second spinning along the narrow street. Colored smoke started spitting into the night air.

"Move where?" Spence demanded.

"Where do you think?" Bolan asked, pointing toward the building where the bulk of the incoming fire was emanating from. "You said we needed to bring a gift, right? Well, how about we give your friends the best gift of all—dead enemies."

MACK BOLAN ®
The Executioner

THE EXECUTIONER

DON PENDLETON'S

FINAL ASSAULT

A GOLD EAGLE BOOK FROM

WORLDWIDE.

TORONTO • NEW YORK • LONDON
AMSTERDAM • PARIS • SYDNEY • HAMBURG
STOCKHOLM • ATHENS • TOKYO • MILAN
MADRID • WARSAW • BUDAPEST • AUCKLAND

First edition December 2015

ISBN-13: 978-0-373-64445-2

Special thanks and acknowledgment to
Joshua Reynolds for his contribution to this work.

Final Assault

Recycling programs
for this product may
not exist in your area.

Printed in U.S.A.

Justice is a temporary thing that must at last come to an end; but the conscience is eternal and will never die.
—Martin Luther

Justice may be temporary, but my war against injustice is everlasting.
—Mack Bolan

THE
MACK BOLAN
LEGEND

Nothing less than a war could have fashioned the destiny of the man called Mack Bolan. Bolan earned the Executioner title in the jungle hell of Vietnam.

But this soldier also wore another name—Sergeant Mercy. He was so tagged because of the compassion he showed to wounded comrades-in-arms and Vietnamese civilians.

Mack Bolan's second tour of duty ended prematurely when he was given emergency leave to return home and bury his family, victims of the Mob. Then he declared a one-man war against the Mafia.

He confronted the Families head-on from coast to coast, and soon a hope of victory began to appear. But Bolan had broken society's every rule. That same society started gunning for this elusive warrior—to no avail.

So Bolan was offered amnesty to work within the system against terrorism. This time, as an employee of Uncle Sam, Bolan became Colonel John Phoenix. With a command center at Stony Man Farm in Virginia, he and his new allies—Able Team and Phoenix Force—waged relentless war on a new adversary: the KGB.

But when his one true love, April Rose, died at the hands of the Soviet terror machine, Bolan severed all ties with Establishment authority.

Now, after a lengthy lone-wolf struggle and much soul-searching, the Executioner has agreed to enter an "arm's-length" alliance with his government once more, reserving the right to pursue personal missions in his Everlasting War.

1

The Gulf of Aden

The inflatable rafts glided across the dark water toward the looming bulk of their target. Garrand crouched in the lead raft, eyes on the prize, finger on the trigger. He expected no complications—the plan was solid—but it was best to prepare for trouble.

Georges Garrand always had a plan. It was his compulsion and his pride, and it had seen him through his term of service in the French Foreign Legion in addition to other, less praiseworthy organizations. Be prepared for enemy action and the screwups of your friends, and seize opportunity wherever and whenever you find it.

That motto was the reason Garrand was out here now, riding one of three military surplus boats with twenty of the hardest bastards in his Rolodex, armed to the teeth and high on coffee and ephedrine tablets. That was why he was going to take the *Demeter*.

The world's first self-sustaining vessel, the *Demeter* was a super-yacht. The cargo holds had been converted into, among other things, two decks of passenger cabins, a five-star galley and hydroponic farms. An artificial cove had been built into the forward area of the hull, at the waterline, for fishing. The vessel had roughly 4,300 square feet of solar panels attached to it and an 860-foot skysail, which could be deployed at the touch of a button. A backup diesel engine was located on an engineering deck the size of a small village.

It was a floating city. A small city, true, but worth more money than Garrand had ever seen. And it was his for the taking if his plan went off without a hitch. Which it would, because it was his plan.

Two fingers tapped his shoulder, and he glanced back at his second-in-command, Yacoub. The Moroccan pulled down the edge of his keffiyeh and grinned. "What a way to earn a paycheck, eh, Georges?" Yacoub had served in the Legion with him, and when Garrand had decided to seek larger fortunes for less risk, the other man had come along.

"There are worse ways. And keep your cover on. There are too many cameras on that boat. No sense in giving the game away early." Garrand tugged on his own keffiyeh for emphasis. All of the men in the rafts wore them, along with stripped-down FELIN suits. The electronics had been removed from the flak jackets and they didn't have helmets, but all the men carried FAMAS rifles. The bullpup-style assault rifles were the service weapon of the French military, with a large trigger guard, a STANAG magazine and a handguard just below the muzzle. It was a compact, efficient weapon…two things Garrand prized.

Standardization of equipment was one of Garrand's keystones. If everyone was using the same type of weapon, ammo rationing would be easier. He'd gotten the equipment, and more besides, from a black market dealer who'd owed him a favor or six. An investment in mercy that had paid large dividends.

Their clothing had been dyed and artfully torn in places to give the impression of hard use. Yacoub and several of the others, those who could pass for locals at a distance, had stripped the sleeves from their shirts. Garrand, born and raised in Marseille, kept his sleeves pulled down. The deception wouldn't pass muster with anyone who was halfway knowledgeable about the region, but that wasn't Garrand's problem. It wouldn't matter in the long run, at any rate.

As they drew close to the *Demeter*, he caught the faint sounds of music and laughter from the upper decks, far above his head. Garrand smiled. It was the *Demeter*'s world tour, and besides her crew, guests of every social stripe as well as their hangers-on and members of the press were on board. He had memorized the names and faces and the net worth of each just in case. It always pays to have a backup plan.

"What fool thought this was a good place for a party?" Yacoub asked, shaking his head. "It's like they're begging to be attacked."

"This tub has a security force of thirty, and it's reinforced to the point of ridiculousness. Even the most aggressive pirates couldn't take the *Demeter*," Garrand said. "It's the floating equivalent of a gated community. What better way to show how secure it is than to float right through pirate alley?"

Yacoub shook his head again. "Still seems like asking for trouble to me." He laughed and hefted his assault rifle. "But who am I to judge?"

"We've got a ten-minute window in the Maritime Security Patrol area, so when we have boots on the deck, move quick," Garrand said, looking at the others. "We need to hit them hard and fast before they know what's going on. Take over the control and engine rooms, and that's game, set and match. And keep your cover up. We're being paid to look like pirates, so play pirate. Don't kill anyone you don't have to."

"You sure about the timing?" one of the others grunted. A Serbian named Borjan. Garrand looked at him, and Borjan fell silent. Garrand was touchy about his plans. They all knew that, but it didn't stop some of them from pressing the issue.

"Yes," he said slowly, "I am quite sure." Garrand looked back toward the vessel. "Aim for the cove," he said to the man controlling the tiller. Until recently, he'd been part of the *Demeter*'s security staff, just like everyone on Garrand's team. Garrand himself had been head of security before he and his men were very publicly fired. All part of their employer's plan. It was a good plan. His was better, though. More profitable, too.

The cove was shuttered, as he'd expected. The metal doors could be opened from within when the *Demeter* was anchored, allowing the artificial cove to flood. But it was standard procedure to keep the *Demeter* shuttered tight while in the designated hot spots—the Gulf of Aden, the Strait of Malacca, a few others. Garrand knew this because he'd come up with that policy himself. He also knew the strength of the shutters, having overseen their installation. They would resist most forms of explosive…unless it was attached at just the right point.

"Chuckles," Garrand said. The big American mercenary gave a grunt of acknowledgment and slid to the side of the raft, a shaped charge in his hands. He leaned out and gestured. Garrand nodded. "That's it. Hurry it up. We have a hijacking to get on with."

"Just call me D. B. Cooper," Chuckles said, as he attached the charge to the spot Garrand had indicated. When it exploded, it would disable the shutters' locking mechanism. Without that, the hull would ratchet open.

"I would, but we're not in a plane and you're terrible with parachutes," Garrand said. "Set the damn thing up. We're on a schedule." He signaled for the tillerman to pull the raft back. The explosion wouldn't be large, but no sense tempting fate. Garrand waved the other two rafts back, as well. "Wait…" he said as Chuckles readied the detonator.

"I know, I know," the mercenary replied. Garrand frowned at the edge in the other man's voice; Chuckles was good at his job, but he was testy. He didn't like being told what to do, a trait he shared with the others. As the raft reached a safe distance, Garrand chopped his hand through the air.

"Open sesame," Chuckles said, and the charge went off with a dull *krump*. Metal groaned and water slopped over the sides of the raft as the shutters opened like the petals of a flower.

"Hit it," Garrand barked. The motor growled and

the raft shot forward through the widening gap. As they entered the *Demeter*'s belly, he could hear alarms wailing. He lifted his assault rifle and was already leaping out of the raft as it thudded against the cove's fiberglass shore. The others followed suit and soon, all twenty of his men were moving up the slope.

Garrand saw a startled face peering out through the window of the shutter control booth—the night crew—and fired. The window rattled as the bulletproof glass absorbed his shots, as he'd known it would, but the face vanished. "Two men on duty," he said. "One armed, one not."

"Unless they changed the routine after we left," Yacoub said as they sprinted toward the booth. The others were spreading out, covering the entrance to the cove. They knew what to do and did it with the alacrity of trained professionals. Yacoub and two others would hit the engine room. The rest would follow Garrand to the upper decks and the control center. But first, they had to secure the cove.

"They didn't change anything," Garrand said.

Yacoub fired a burst at the closest set of speakers, mounted above the booth, and cut off one of the sirens in mid-wail. "Eight minutes until our window closes, by the way."

"Plenty of time," Garrand said. He hit the steel door with his boot. "Open up!" He kicked it again and then thumped it with the butt of his weapon.

Silence. That too was standard procedure. One member of the security team and a crewmember would be on duty. The booth was reinforced, and theoretically, the men inside could wait out most anything, up to and including an assault by armed invaders. Theoretically. Yacoub made a face. "Want to blow it open?"

Even as he spoke, a muffled sound came from within. "No need," Garrand said. He waved Yacoub back as the lock disengaged and the door swung open. A man wearing the gray fatigues of the *Demeter*'s security forces stepped out of the booth holding a smoking pistol. "Hello, Sergei. How's tricks?" Garrand asked mildly.

"Better now," Sergei said. The big Russian was slab-faced, with eyes like polished stones. Beneath the plain uniform his broad torso was covered in elaborate tattoos. Sergei looked at Yacoub and nodded.

"Sergei," Yacoub replied. The two men eyed one another for a moment and then looked away. They didn't like each other, but they were professionals. They would work together. Failing that, he'd shoot one of them. He peered past Sergei into the control booth. He saw a body on the floor and blood. He looked at Sergei questioningly.

"I let him get off an alert, as you asked," Sergei said.

"Pirates?"

"I told him you were the most piratical Somalis to ever prowl these waters," Sergei said, holstering his weapon. He glanced toward the cove and then cocked an ear to the alarms. "Speaking of which, that hole in the hull is going to be a red flag to the bastards when they figure out we're dead in the water. Those alarms will carry for miles, and even the most pig-ignorant fisherman knows what that sound means by now."

"And that's why you're here, Sergei." Garrand

smiled and clapped him on the shoulder. "Make sure no one else tries to steal this boat before I do."

"I'm going to need more men," Sergei said doubtfully.

"I know," Garrand said. His smile turned wolfish. "Don't worry, Sergei—it's all part of the plan."

2

The Biggest Little City in the World

The Catania Hotel in Reno, Nevada, had seen better decades. The upper floors had been stripped to the plaster for everything and anything that could be sold, and the bottom floors weren't much better. It had been five years since a guest had stayed at the hotel. These days, the only resident was a certain representative of the Claricuzio family and his bodyguards.

Mack Bolan, aka the Executioner, gave a quiet grunt of effort as he inserted the crowbar between the doors of the elevator. The elevator hadn't gone higher than the sixth floor since the upper floors had been stripped, and the car was permanently stationed on the third for the exclusive use of Domingo Claricuzio and his bodyguards. Bracing his foot against the wall, Bolan forced the doors open and peered down into the shaft.

Bolan, clad in khaki fatigues and body armor,

tossed the crowbar aside and swiftly slid a safety harness over the rest of his gear. A Heckler & Koch UMP-45 was strapped across his chest and his KA-BAR combat knife sat snugly in its sheath on his leg. After he'd gotten the harness on, he clipped several M-18 smoke grenades to lanyards for easy access.

It had been simple enough to get onto the Catania's roof from the casino next door; Domingo had neglected to post guards on the upper floors. Perhaps the elderly *don* thought he didn't need to bother with such measures.

Bolan hefted an ascender—the same device used by repair technicians—and attached it to the elevator cable and his harness. Then he clipped his harness to the cable and took a slow breath. His heart rate was steady. Instinctively, he checked his harness and his gear once more, and then, with a sound like tearing silk, he began to descend the length of the shaft.

Despite being semiretired and in hiding from his enemies, Claricuzio had his fingers in more than one greasy pie. He ran any number of businesses at a remove, including some profitable prostitution rings in Eastern Europe and the Mediterranean. But not for much longer.

At that thought, Bolan's sun-bronzed face split in a grim smile. In the earliest days of his long and bloody war, he'd gunned down men like Domingo by the dozen and had taken his own licks in turn. Bullets, blackjacks and blades had exacted a cruel toll from his flesh over the years, and he sometimes wondered if he were held together by nothing more than scar tissue and bone sutures. But it was all worth it, every moment of blood and pain. When beasts like Claricuzio were put down, lives were saved—the lives they would have ruined or tainted or ended.

The Executioner had needed only a few days to set everything up. He'd kept tabs on his target, and he knew the hotel's layout down to the unconnected light switch on the first floor. Five guards were posted at any one time: one in Claricuzio's suite, two on the hall doors and two more patrolling the floors above and below, respectively. If any of Claricuzio's brood were visiting, there might be more, but the don's family members weren't the visiting types. Even so, there was a chance Bolan would be facing more resistance than just five inattentive and relatively lazy punks in bad suits, which meant he would have to be quick and careful. Even a punk could get lucky.

On that grim note, the soles of his boots touched the top of the elevator. Swiftly he disengaged his harness and dropped to his haunches. With the tip of his combat knife, he pried up the hatch and dropped through. Bolan disabled the control panel and pulled a small wedge of thick rubber from his harness. Holding it between his teeth, he carefully pried open the elevator doors and slid the wedge into the gap to hold the doors open. Next, Bolan removed a small dental mirror from a pocket, unfolded it and slid it through the gap at the bottom of the doors.

Angling it one way and then the other, he pinpointed the two guards in the hall. Bolan retracted the mirror, placed it in his pocket and pulled a smoke grenade from his harness. He hauled the doors open with one hand and popped the pin on the grenade. Then he rolled the canister down the corridor, where it hissed and spewed smoke.

Shouts of alarm cut the air. Bolan sent another grenade rolling down the hall in the opposite direction. When the corridor was filled with smoke, he stepped out. The soldier knew there were a number of possible responses to the tactic he'd just employed. Men with training, or an iota of common sense, might sit tight and call for backup. But the men Domingo Claricuzio had paid to keep him safe were neither trained nor sensible. They would either blunder into the smoke or—

Italian loafers scuffed the carpet. A man coughed and cursed. Bolan caught a blindly reaching hand and drove a fist into the exposed elbow. Bone snapped and the guard screamed. Bolan lifted a boot and slammed it down onto a vulnerable patella. The kneecap slid and cracked beneath the blow, and Bolan grabbed the screaming man by his lapels and whirled him around.

The guard jerked as a pistol snarled. Shooting blind was the other possibility. Bolan held the dying man upright and reached across his chest to grab the pistol holstered beneath the guard's cheap jacket. Without pulling the gun from its holster, he twisted it up and got a grip on the butt. Then he charged forward, holding up the sagging weight of the dead man like a shield. The smoke billowed and swirled, parted by the abrupt motion. He saw the second guard, eyes wide, mouth agape, the black-barrelled automatic in his hand bobbing up to fire again. Bolan fired first. The rounds punched through its previous owner's coat and perforated the skull of the guard who'd killed him. He fell back against the door to the stairs, a red halo marking the wall behind his head.

Bolan let his human shield drop and he spun, raising the UMP. He fired off a burst, chewing the frame of the door that led to Claricuzio's rooms. The door, which had been in the process of opening, slammed shut. Bolan didn't hesitate. He padded forward quickly, aware that the other two guards could show up at any time. He fired two quick bursts with the UMP, once where the lock would be and then where the hinges would be screwed into the frame. Then he hit the door with his shoulder and rode it down. His teeth rattled in his head as he landed but it was better than having them shot out of his head by the guard he knew was inside the room.

The latter let off a panicked shot that sliced the air above Bolan's head, then fell screaming as the soldier cut his legs out from under him with a burst from the UMP. Bolan pushed himself to his feet and stepped fully into the room, pausing only to deliver the coup de grace to the wounded man.

Domingo Claricuzio sat in his chair, his eyes on the television in front of him. He looked like an elderly hawk, and any excess flesh he might have once possessed had sloughed off with the passage of years. Claricuzio was a dangerous man, quick with a blade or a garrotte even into his sixties. "I like this show," Claricuzio said, apropos of nothing. He pulled his feet back as the blood from his guard soaked into the carpet. His gaze flicked to the dead man. He clucked his tongue. "His mother will be disappointed."

His eyes tilted, taking in Bolan and the smoking weapon he cradled. "I expected you sooner." It was said calmly. There was no fear or anger or hate in the old man's eyes, just…nothing. It was like looking into the eyes of a shark.

Bolan stared at the old man silently. This was not what he'd expected. He had come intending to cut the head off a snake, but taking the mobster into custody would be just as effective.

"Get up," he said. "You have a gun?"

Claricuzio made a face. "Do I have a gun? What do I look like?" he said.

A shout from behind propelled Bolan into motion, and with instinct born from painful experience he hurled himself to the side. The soldier crashed into the wall and used the momentum to spin himself around as a flurry of bullets cracked through the air where he'd been standing.

Claricuzio gave a shout and flung himself out of his chair. Bolan couldn't take the time to track him. His trigger finger twitched, and he emptied the UMP's clip into the first of the gunmen who'd entered the room behind him.

The second, whether through desperation or simple instinct, lunged past his compatriot's falling body and crashed into Bolan. The Executioner let the UMP drop and grabbed his opponent's wrist, twisting the black shape of the automatic up and away from his face. The gunman cursed him in Italian and hammered a punch into his side. Bolan barely felt it, thanks to his body armor. He smashed his forearm into the guard's face as he squeezed the man's wrist, forcing him to release his pistol. As the gun clattered to the floor, he jerked the man's arm up and drove his fist into the fleshy point where arm met shoulder. The guard's arm dislocated with an audible *pop* and he stumbled back, his face white with pain. Bolan didn't let him get far.

He grabbed the guard's shirt, whirled him about and snaked his arms around the man's neck, snapping it. Bolan let the body topple forward and released a sharp breath.

Something dug into Bolan's side. It didn't penetrate his body armor, but it took the wind out of him. If Bolan hadn't been wearing the armor, he would have been dead. The soldier twisted about, clawing for his knife as Claricuzio came at him again. "You asked if I had a gun. I don't, but I got a knife, and I know just where to put it," he said as he slashed at Bolan with a thin, medieval-looking stiletto. "You think you can just show up and take me down?"

"That was the plan," Bolan said, backing away, one hand extended to block Claricuzio's next blow. As he spoke, he drew his KA-BAR combat knife and held it low.

"Who sent you, hey? Anthony? Salvatore?" Claricuzio licked his lips. "Little Sasha?"

"None of the above," Bolan said.

Claricuzio shook his head irritably. "You'll tell me," he said. He lunged, moving with the grace of a man half his age, almost quicker than Bolan's eye could follow. The tip of the stiletto scratched a red line across Bolan's chin as he ducked his head to protect his throat. The soldier drove his own knife into Claricuzio's side, angling the blade toward the heart. The old mafioso stumbled against him with a strangled wheeze. Bolan extricated himself and the other man slid off his knife and tumbled to the floor.

He sank to his haunches beside Claricuzio but didn't bother to check for a pulse. The old man was dead. Bolan's knife had torn through his heart, and his blood was soaking into the floorboards, where it mingled with that of his guards. Bolan examined the withered features for a moment, then looked away. Claricuzio had deserved death, and he'd gotten it. The Executioner pushed himself to his feet and snatched up the UMP. It was time to go. The police likely wouldn't arrive for some time, but there was no reason to tempt fate.

Bolan's sat phone rang.

His mind considered and discarded possibilities in the millisecond between the second ring and the moment he accepted the call and raised the phone to his ear. "All finished, Striker?"

"Yes."

"Good." There was a brief hesitation. "Claricuzio—I don't have to ask, I suppose."

Something in Hal Brognola's tone caused Bolan to snap alert. "What is it?"

"The usual," Brognola said grimly.

Bolan looked at the bodies at his feet and said, "Talk."

3

The Gulf of Aden

"There he is," Yacoub said softly. He made a surreptitious gesture toward the sky and the black shape moving through its wide, blue expanse.

Garrand glanced up and then back at his watch. He, Yacoub and three of his men stood on the *Demeter*'s upper deck, between the control room and what Garrand thought of as the cabana—a sheltered wet bar and outdoor swimming pool.

"Right on time," he said. Ten hours had passed since they'd stormed the ship. The plan had gone off without a hitch, as he'd known it would. Though there were a few bodies to be disposed of, once they had time. He tapped his watch. "I'll say this for him—he's prompt."

"He better be. I'm getting tired of standing out here in the sun so the remoras can film us," Yacoub said, jerking the barrel of his weapon toward the gaggle of hostages corralled in the cabana. They were mostly press, with a few others mixed in—whose names and faces Garrand found vaguely familiar. Celebrities with nothing better to do than ride around on a retro-fitted cargo ship, including three reality show final-ists, an advice columnist and one style blogger, none of whom seemed to really understand their predica-ment. Or if they did, they were hiding it well.

Garrand smiled. He'd allowed the press to keep their cameras, and they had repaid him with a con-stant stream of camera flashes, equipment squawks and shouted questions. *All part of the plan,* he re-minded himself as he watched the helicopter draw closer.

"I wonder where he got a helicopter," Yacoub mur-mured. "Sure as hell not Eyl," he added after a min-ute.

"Yemen," Garrand said, shifting his rifle to a more comfortable position. "He has a finger in every pie." He tugged at his keffiyeh, wanting a cigarette. Sweat rolled down under his collar. It was hot, and he was getting tired of playing pirate. He glanced at the hos-tages. They'd selected eight out of the twenty passen-gers—the most attractive and the most important. This was a photo opportunity, after all. The rest had been sealed below decks with the crew. *Well, most of the crew,* he thought with a satisfied sigh.

The *Demeter* had a crew of sixty, thirty of whom were security personnel. Of the thirty, only five weren't in on the plan. Those five had been confined with the others after judicious application of rifle butts, fists and boots. Garrand had hired most of the security men himself, specifically for this trip, before his very public firing. *Who fires somebody on Twitter?* he thought. He didn't even have an account. But that was a silly question. Nicholas Alva Pierpoint was *exactly* the sort of man who'd fire someone via social media.

"Helicopter's not going to land," Yacoub said.

"The pilot's no fool," Garrand replied. "Would you land a chopper on the deck of a ship swarming with guys wearing these—" he tugged on his keffiyeh "—and carrying automatic weapons?"

Yacoub laughed. "I suppose not."

"Besides, you remember how Pierpoint likes to make an entrance." Garrand pointed at the helicopter, which was now passing overhead. "And there he is now—the sixth most powerful man on the planet."

As they watched, a tiny figure flung itself out of the helicopter and plummeted toward the *Demeter*. A rectangular parachute popped open and slowed the man's descent. Yacoub whistled softly, and Garrand shook his head.

As expected, the hostages were filming the new arrival. At least one of them had managed to maintain a live feed of the "unfolding situation," thanks to Garrand ensuring that the onboard wireless network was functioning. Garrand had no doubt that every news agency—legitimate, tabloid or otherwise—was salivating over the whole affair in real time. *When in doubt, make news,* he thought. That was one of Pierpoint's guiding philosophies, right alongside "all publicity is good publicity."

Well, he was getting both in spades with this one. One of his men halfheartedly raised his weapon and for a second, Garrand contemplated letting him get a shot off. Then he gestured sharply. The barrel of the rifle was lowered and Pierpoint landed light as a cat on the deck. Clad in black, he was dressed like a little boy playing war. Pierpoint was small and sandy haired and was wearing wraparound shades. Garrand thought he looked a little like a certain American movie star, the one who'd made that film about bartenders and liked to stand on couches. With an elegant flick of his fingers, Pierpoint snapped the deflated parachute loose from his harness and let the wind carry it out to sea.

"How did he manage to land with the sun at his back? That's what I want to know," Yacoub muttered. "Did someone teach him how to do that, or—"

"Quiet," Garrand said. "The cameras are rolling, and the star has made his entrance."

Pierpoint looked around, hands half raised. "Who's in charge here?" he called out. Pierpoint wasn't American, but he'd hired people to make him sound as nonthreatening as possible to his North American business partners. His nondescript accent rolled off his tongue, smooth as cream.

Garrand nudged Yacoub. "Go get him."

"Why me?"

"You look more like a pirate than I do. Go," Garrand said. He watched in satisfaction as Yacoub stumped across the deck, weapon held across his chest. Camera phones whirred and clicked, and the world watched as Pierpoint met the pirates.

"I've come to talk," Pierpoint said loudly, playing to the cheap seats. "And to see that no one gets hurt." He patted his chest, where a heavy duffel was slung. "I've got the ransom here."

"We talk, then," Yacoub replied in what was not a Somali accent, or even remotely close. *Irish,* Garrand wondered. *Maybe Scottish?* He rolled his eyes and fell in behind Pierpoint as Yacoub strutted toward the stairs.

The control room was occupied by two of Garrand's men, who'd been watching Pierpoint's arrival through the windows. Garrand hiked his thumb over his shoulder as they entered, and the men filed out. They would take his and Yacoub's place on deck and pose for the cameras. Garrand took the captain's chair before Pierpoint could reach it and gestured to one of the lower seats. "Sit. Yacoub, see if anyone is near the galley. A few bottles of champagne were chilling, last I checked. And grab some glasses, as well." He nodded at Pierpoint. "This is a celebration, after all."

Pierpoint smiled widely, displaying expensive dental work. He clapped his hands together and laughed. Garrand tugged his keffiyeh down and grinned. "I told you it would work."

"And that's why I hired you, Georges," Pierpoint said. He swung his feet onto a control panel and leaned back. "Remind me to send a thank you card to your previous employer for the recommendation."

"Given that he's in prison now, I doubt he'd appreciate the sentiment." Garrand sat back. Byron Cloud, his former boss, had been an arms dealer. He'd hired Garrand to put the boot to his competition, at a verifiable remove. Garrand had spent two weeks sinking boats full of secondhand military equipment in the South China Sea. A fun way to spend one's time, but there was little future in the field of hard sabotage;

these days it was all about computers and accounts and data tracking.

Pierpoint laughed. "Poor Byron—bit of a wet noodle, that fellow," he said.

Garrand shrugged. *Whatever that means,* he thought. "You have the money? I've got half a dozen very twitchy shooters wondering when they're getting paid for this little stunt." It wasn't quite as fraught as he made it sound, but it was close. None of his men were what one could call nice, but so far they'd been professional, and that was more important as far as Garrand was concerned.

Pierpoint patted the duffel he'd brought with him. He'd taken it off and was cradling it in his lap. "It's all here. The most generous severance package I've ever provided, if I do say so myself."

"And we're worth every penny," Garrand said. He shook his head. "Still, hijacking your own boat just to raise your profile seems excessive. Especially if you're trying to get investors interested."

"Ah, Georges, that's because you have no idea how brand awareness works. People like narrative— *stories*—more than they like charts and statistics. Give them a good story and they'll throw more money at you than you can handle. The best way to convince potential investors of the merits of my design is to show them how much people want it."

"Yeah, but…pirates?"

"Pirates are hip," Pierpoint said with a shrug. "They're in the public consciousness right now, and it makes for a better story. I look like a hero, the public clamors for information about my recycled superyacht, and the money pours in." Yacoub returned with a bottle of champagne and two glasses. He set it on the control panel and used his knife to pop the cork. Pierpoint accepted a glass and took a swig.

Garrand took his own glass and said, "I can't imagine that super-yachts are a—what do you call it?—growth industry."

"Not even close. But if I have my way, the *Demeter* will be one of a kind," Pierpoint said, chuckling. "Damn boat cost me an arm and a leg to build, not to mention outfit. The component parts are more valuable than the whole, in this instance. The *Demeter* was just about showing what those components could accomplish when brought together. There are hundreds of applications for the technologies aboard this vessel. Everything from sustainable off-shore hydroponics facilities, to green engines, to manmade reefs and shoals that can replace those lost to pollution."

"So this thing is—what? A marketing stunt?" Garrand said.

"I prefer to think of it as an exercise in synergistic brand building," Pierpoint said. "This ship is, frankly, useless. It's too expensive for any individual to maintain, and who needs a yacht with a hydroponics garden? It's a very expensive floating island, and as I already own several islands, I look forward to rendering this boat down to its component parts once this cruise is finished."

"It seems a shame. This vessel has a lot of potential." Garrand looked around.

"Oh?"

"Oh indeed. A few days in the right port of call, and we could turn this thing into the largest drug lab this side of the poppy fields of Afghanistan. Or more…it's a veritable citadel. Self-sustaining, fast and with enough room for a small army. Imagine what mischief the wrong sort of person could get up to with a ship like this—smuggling, drug-running, piracy…" Garrand trailed off. Pierpoint was staring at him. "What?"

"Nothing. Sometimes I forget that you and I have very different social circles, is all."

Garrand snorted. "Not so different as all that." He took a swig of champagne. "You know, I could take it off your hands, if you like."

"What?"

"The *Demeter*," Garrand said. "Since you're only going to strip it for spare parts, you might as well give it to me, no?"

"What—just sell it to you?"

Garrand laughed. "Who said anything about selling?" Pierpoint made to rise to his feet, but Garrand was quicker. He drew his pistol from the holster beneath his arm and pointed it at his former employer, even as he took another sip of champagne. He smacked his lips. "This really is quite good."

"You're double-crossing me," Pierpoint said, bewildered. He settled back into his seat, face pale, hands trembling.

"Technically, I'm simply amending the deal," Garrand said. He holstered his pistol and poured himself another glass of champagne. "I've done all that we agreed to, Nick—may I call you Nick?" Garrand smiled and emptied the glass. "I organized this— what do you call it?—'viral marketing stunt' for your 'brand,'" he said, crooking his fingers in air quotes, "and now I am taking my pay."

"The money was your pay," Pierpoint said through clenched teeth.

"The money was a guarantor of the safety of your guests and crew. The *Demeter* is my pay, and as she is now mine, I intend to sell her for several times what you're worth. In fact, a number of interested parties are already on their way here." Garrand made to fill his glass again, then thought better of it and simply took a swig from the bottle.

Pierpoint stared at him. "You can't…"

"I already have," Garrand said. "It's not so bad, Nick. Think of the marketing possibilities… 'The ship so popular, even criminals want one.' It'll play well, I think." Garrand shrugged. "Or not. I admit, that sort of thing is outside of my area of expertise." He nodded at Yacoub. "Would you be so kind as to take Mr. Pierpoint to his quarters? I think he's going to need a few hours to recover."

Garrand watched Pierpoint go and then took another swig from the bottle. He'd played it cool, but he was all too aware that he'd entered a less structured area of the plan. There were more balls in the air, more things that could go wrong at this stage. But the rewards were greater, as well.

He pulled the duffel to him, unzipped it and examined the plastic-wrapped bundles of cash. Then he grunted and zipped it back up. It was a good amount of money, but the boat would bring more. A lot more, if he played his cards right. "People like narrative," he murmured.

The hostages were no longer bargaining chips. Instead, now they were insurance—as long as the usual suspects thought there was a chance of keeping them alive, they would hold off from any action. Not for long, of course. But long enough. He'd already adapted the cover story—they were no longer pirates, but terrorists seeking to make a statement—and he'd organized the appropriate means of disguising the arrival of his guests. But it was still a matter of timing and precision.

Garrand finished the champagne and set it aside. "Let the show begin," he murmured.

4

Somewhere South of Yemen

The Executioner had found a number of papers among the late Domingo Claricuzio's effects—including those naming the men in charge of Claricuzio's Mediterranean operations. Enforced prostitution, human trafficking, the works... Bolan itched to bring the whole operation down.

But that would have to wait. Instead, he was on an unlisted flight. The plane was private, bankrolled on a black ops budget and stuffed to the gills with enough hardware to make it look like the set of a science fiction film. Bolan sat alongside Hal Brognola and three others in the plane's state-of-the-art passenger compartment. They were heading toward the gulf, as near as Bolan could tell.

Brognola looked tired. Then, he always looked tired. As director of the ultrasecret antiterrorist Sensitive Operations Group, Brognola got his orders from the President himself.

Bolan looked around. Computer screens lined the cabin, resting above banks of hardware, including what he recognized as control consoles for drones and remote satellite surveillance systems. There were no windows, and the cabin had the blocky design he'd come to associate with stealth vehicles. He could hear the purr of the engines and the soft conversation of the crew. The internal lighting was cold, blue and sterile and it cast chilly shadows across the faces of the men around him.

Bolan knew for a fact one of the men was well out of his jurisdiction. He was African-American with hard features, and his scalp stubble was gray. Bolan met his bland gaze and said, "Still with the Bureau, Ferguson? Or have you traded down and joined the Agency?" He'd first made Ferguson's acquaintance when a group of psychotic white supremacists had attempted to loose an antediluvian plague. Bolan had tracked them halfway to the Arctic Circle before he could put paid to the threat they represented, with a little help from the FBI.

"He speaks," Ferguson said. "And it's only been, what, three hours since we left Dulles?" He looked at the others and shrugged. "Can you believe this guy?"

"How do you know he has not joined Interpol, hey, Cooper?" one of the others said, leaning forward. Slim and dark, he wore an Italian suit.

Brognola laughed. "Agent Cooper knows better than that, Chantecoq."

Bolan had first met the French Interpol agent and his subordinate, Tanzir, during a terrorist attempt to enter the United States through Mexico. "How is Agent Tanzir?" Bolan asked, looking at Chantecoq.

"Very well, Cooper," Chantecoq said. Bolan inclined his head and looked at the third man. Tall and blunt featured with an expensive haircut and even more expensive sunglasses.

"CIA," the Executioner said without hesitation.

"Among others," the third man replied. He smiled and extended his hand. "My name's Tony Spence. Pleasure to meet you, Agent Cooper. Big fan of your work." All of the men present, save Brognola, knew Bolan by his cover identity, Agent Matt Cooper. Bolan had used many names throughout his long, lonely war, and he suspected that he would use many more before the end. Each name was like a weapon in his arsenal, opening doors and armoring him against the slings and arrows of his enemies.

Bolan didn't take his hand. "I knew Tony Spence. He had about twenty pounds on you, and you've got about six inches on him. And he's dead." Spence had been Bolan's CIA contact for a recent mission to Hong Kong—a mission that had gone dangerously wrong at the eleventh hour. Spence retracted his hand.

"He is. I'm not," he said, still smiling. Bolan frowned. He had a long, complex relationship with various agents of the CIA. Some of his interactions had fallen somewhere on the spectrum between frustration and anger, but he'd grown to like Spence—the original Spence—in the brief time he'd known him.

"You can let me off at the next airport," Bolan said. "I've got more important things to do than waste my time playing games."

Brognola cleared his throat. "Ease back, Cooper.

You know how these Puzzle Palace types like to complicate things. Every one of them has three names and none of them the one their momma gave them. Tony Spence is just an alias for use by whoever needs it at the moment."

Spence inclined his head. "And right now, that's me."

Bolan sat back. He looked around. "CIA, FBI and Interpol…something smells funny."

"Might be my aftershave. Wife's making me try something new," Ferguson said.

Brognola shook his head. "If you think those are the only letters in this particular alphabet soup, I've got some bad news…" He held up a hand as if to forestall the protest Bolan hadn't been planning to make. "But that's beside the point. What do you know from yachts, Cooper?"

"Been on a few," Bolan said without elaborating.

"What about cargo ships?" Spence asked, leaning forward.

"Been on a few of those, too."

"What do you know about—"

Bolan cut Spence off with an impatient gesture. "Pretend I don't, since you seem to want to tell me a story," he said curtly.

Spence smirked. He turned in his seat and pointed to one of the screens that lined the cabin as he tapped at a tablet. The volume increased, and Bolan found himself watching a BBC news report on an ongoing hostage situation somewhere in the Gulf of Aden. "Pirates," he said. He'd dealt with modern pirates before, both in Somali waters and in the South China Sea. The former were mostly fishermen, out of their depth and desperate. The latter tended toward smuggling and drug running.

"So they'd have you think," Brognola said. Bolan glanced at him. "Well, they might have been pirates to begin with, but they're claiming to be terrorists right now. They might be something else tomorrow."

"It's not the pirates we're worried about," Ferguson said. He made a face. "Show him, Spence." Spence tapped the tablet again, and a recording began to play on the screen. It was the same ship, Bolan saw, only from a different angle. He squinted.

"Camera phone?" he asked.

"These pirates are very social-media friendly," Chantecoq murmured.

As Bolan watched, a man parachuted toward the deck. Spence froze the image and zoomed in on the parachutist's face. "Recognize him, Cooper?" Brognola asked.

Bolan shook his head.

"Nicholas Alva Pierpoint. Sustainable technologies wunderkind," Brognola supplied.

"Never heard of him," Bolan said.

"If you had, I'd be more upset than I am now," Brognola said drily. "He decided to make a public display of idiocy and parachuted onto his own hijacked ship to deliver the ransom, despite the collective scream of his lawyers." Bolan watched as Pierpoint was led away. Brognola sighed. "Turned out the bloodsuckers were right for once. It was a singularly bad idea, and Pierpoint got added to the hostages, whereupon our merry band of pirates revealed that they were terrorists, and they'd trade the hostages for the release of certain prisoners in the usual places—Guantanamo Bay, Israel, Nigeria."

"Any pattern?" Bolan asked.

"None. We think somebody picked names out of a hat and went for broke."

"So it's a scam. What do they really want?"

"Near as we can figure, to sell the ship to the highest bidder. And in fact, a number of said bidders have shown up. We've got surveillance footage from various ports of call, including Hargeisa International Airport, and a drone spotted the whole lot of potential buyers a few hours ago—guess where?—being welcomed aboard the *Demeter*." Spence brought a number of grainy pictures onto the screen. One was of an antiquated speedboat hurtling across the water. There were several figures in it.

"You recognize this guy, I'm sure." Spence zoomed in on one of the men in the boat. He was a big man with a round face and double chin. But he had a strangler's hands, crisscrossed with scar tissue. The man's name was Gribov, and he was an ex-KGB operative. Gribov, like a lot of former KGB men, had found new employment with a group of Pacific gangsters called the Yellow Chrysanthemum.

Bolan stared at the broad, squashed face of the notorious killer. "Who else?" he said.

"S. M. Kravitz," Spence continued, tapping the tablet. The image of Gribov pixilated and was replaced by that of a thin man in an expensive suit with hair the color of sand and eyeglasses so thick a welder could have used them. He was walking through an airport. "Until recently, he was one of the money men for the Society of Thylea, as well as half a dozen other

European right-wing organizations. God only knows who he's working for now, since the Society got rolled up, but he's here and looking altogether uncomfortable, what with all the armed brown folks."

Bolan grimaced at the mention of the Society of Thylea. Gribov was a killer, but the Society was worse, wanting to wipe out two-thirds of the human population. He'd seen to their destruction personally, although both Ferguson and Chantecoq had, in their own ways, helped.

"This handsome fellow is Walid Nur-al Din," Spence said as Kravitz's lean shape was replaced by a Middle Eastern man dressed in battered fatigues and body armor and climbing out of a truck. His face was marred by an oddly geometric pattern of scars. "Syrian, mouthpiece of the Black Mountain Caliphate, one of several splinter groups of ISIL still fighting in Syria. Nearly got his face peeled off by a Bouncing Betty a few years ago, which did not improve his general temperament." Spence tapped the tablet again.

"And finally, representing the Black Serpent Society, Mr. Drenk." Drenk was Eurasian and, like Gribov and Kravitz, dressed as if he were heading to a boardroom, rather than the deck of a recently hijacked ship. He was walking along the shore toward a waiting boat. "Drenk is a nasty customer—they're all nasty customers, but Drenk is the worst—with a file so thick we couldn't bring it on the plane for the weight limit. Drenk isn't known for his negotiating skills, so God only knows what he's planning."

Spence looked up from his tablet. "Those are the ones who took the bait. Garrand—the man who's leading the terrorists—has four potential bidders, and we can't allow any of them to take possession of the *Demeter*."

"Why?"

"The *Demeter* is one of a kind. Lots of hush-hush goodies went into that particular basket—green technologies, mostly, things that'll make a lot of the usual suspects angry, when and if they permeate the corporate membrane," Spence said.

"You make it sound as if this Pierpoint had some covert help," Bolan said. "That's it, isn't it? All that technology—it was government funded, wasn't it?"

Spence shrugged. "Partially, and through third parties, most of whom have an interest in seeing the United States of America weaned off foreign oil. Pierpoint's smart. He knows the ship is a good way of showing off all these previously underfunded projects in one fancy package. Once the money starts coming in, that tub will be stripped for salvage quicker than sin. The problem is, nobody bothered to file off the serial numbers."

Bolan laughed. There was precious little mirth in the sound. "You're afraid that if the ship falls into the wrong hands, people will—what?—figure out that the federal government was slipping a few extra bucks to Pierpoint under the table in a bid to undercut certain major industrial concerns?"

Spence looked at Brognola. "You were right. He's clever."

"No, just experienced," Bolan said. He shook his head. "And it's not a good enough reason. So elaborate."

"Fine, you want more? Imagine what a savage like Gribov could do with a ship like that. Or Walid. You a movie fan, Cooper? Rule one—never give a super-vehicle to a bad guy. Especially when the vehicle in question is an ocean-going fortress. Which the *Demeter* is. It can sit out of sight in international waters forever, like the goddamn Flying Dutchman, only instead of ghostly sailors it has a crew of Jihadists or gunrunners or revolutionaries. All three maybe—that's the worst-case scenario."

Bolan was silent. The thought was not a pleasant one, he had to admit. Whoever got the ship would be in possession of a state-of-the-art vessel. Brognola cleared his throat. He looked uncomfortable, and Bolan wondered how much pressure he was under to help clean up this mess. "If there were anyone else capable of doing this, Cooper, I'd have dealt them in. But everyone is up to their bootlaces in blood and bullets, and this needs handling soon," Brognola said.

"How many hostages?" Bolan asked after a minute. That was his main concern. The men and women on the *Demeter*, crew included, were innocent, and Bolan was determined to see them to safety, if possible.

"At least twenty passengers, but we're not sure how many crewmembers are helping the kidnappers and how many might have been imprisoned. That's not counting Pierpoint himself."

Bolan sat back. In truth, he had decided to take the assignment the minute Brognola had asked him, such was his respect for the other man. But he needed to know the stakes before he went in. "So you'd like me to free the hostages and take the ship back." Bolan examined the schematics Spence had brought up on the screen, his mind already pinpointing important

areas. He wondered how many men the criminal bidders had brought—potentially three or four apiece,
at least, if whoever was in charge was stupid enough
to allow them to bring bodyguards. That meant the
enemies could number fifty or more. He'd faced long
odds before, but rarely like this.

"No, we'd like you to scuttle it, frankly." Spence
made a face. "Pierpoint messed up, and so did we
when we trusted him not to. Best for everybody if
we wipe the board clean."

"Best for you, you mean," Bolan said. Spence
shrugged.

"To-may-to, toh-mah-to," he said, smiling. Bolan
didn't like that smile, but there were innocent people to think about, and he was going to need help to
get them out alive. If that included Spence, so be it.

"What do we know about the hijackers?" Bolan
asked. "Whose flag are they flying?"

Chantecoq cleared his throat. "They're not terrorists, no matter how they're dressed. We know that
much." He handed Bolan several files and a handful
of grainy photographs. "We caught faces with that last
drone survey. They're careful, but after a few days,
even the most careful are due a slip. Their leader is
suspected to be Georges Garrand. Former member
of the Foreign Legion, former contractor for several
Eastern European governments, including a leader
currently in exile. Until recently, he was employed
by Pierpoint Solutions as a security consultant. He
was responsible for most of the security measures on
the ship. Pierpoint fired him personally just after the
Demeter set sail."

"Fired him?" Bolan asked.

"By social media, no less. For all the world to see," Chantecoq said, gesturing grandly. He smiled thinly. "Clever, no?"

Bolan didn't reply. He flipped through the file. It was nothing he hadn't seen before. Garrand was a mercenary. A very effective mercenary, but then, he'd fought those more than once. Still, Garrand was no thug—he was a decorated soldier with medals for bravery and a reputation for getting the job done. It was clear that Garrand was no saint, but neither was he the sort of man content to play hired gun for very long. As Bolan scanned the papers and photos, the meaning behind Chantecoq's words finally registered. He looked up. "He was fired publicly? Why?" Bolan answered his own question a half second later. "To divert suspicion that this was an inside job."

"That's the working theory," Ferguson said, running his palms over his head. "We've had Pierpoint's domestic operations under investigation for several months. When we started looking into the *Demeter* project, it rang all sorts of bells. Too many wrong names too close to a project like this."

Bolan nodded. "Like Garrand."

"And a few others," Ferguson said. "All of whom have records longer than my arm. Once we started digging into them—and *Demeter*…"

"It alerted us," Chantecoq finished. "We are very interested in Mr. Garrand. He's on our list. So we started to investigate as well, which alerted our American cousins." He gestured to Spence.

"And here we are," Spence said, spreading his hands. "Bouncing a hot potato back and forth until it landed in Hal's lap. Sorry, Hal," Spence added. He didn't sound sorry.

Bolan resisted the urge to shake his head. All these government agencies only seemed to make the situation more and more complicated.

"Stuff your sorries in a sack," Brognola grunted as he shoved an unlit cigar between his teeth.

"So, what do you want from me?" Bolan asked.

"We've got a boat that's too high profile to stay above the water line, full of hostages and crewed by the lost and the damned," Spence said. "Saturday morning serial territory, huh, Cooper?"

"Depends. How am I getting on the *Demeter*—jet pack?" Bolan asked, already thinking. He would need explosives, not many, placed at the correct points. Every structure had its weak spots, and the *Demeter* was no different. Once the ship started taking on water—

"Ha! No," Spence said. He brought up a map and tapped a dot on the screen. Bolan recognized the Somali coastline. "This is Radbur. Old town on the coast of the Republic of Somaliland. Right on the Gulf of Aden, within spitting distance of our merry band of hijackers and the *Demeter*. Mostly fishermen. And these days, where there are fishermen, there'll be pirates."

"And you happen to know one of these pirates?"

"Indeed I do," Spence said. "His name is Axmed. He was a pirate before it was popular and a smuggler in the off season. The Somaliland Navy has a price on his head, as do the Ethiopians, but he's a relatively friendly guy."

"Relatively?" Bolan asked.

Spence ignored him. "Axmed owes me one. If I know him like I think I do, he's been eyeing the *Demeter* all this time. Hell, he's probably already planning to try for it, especially given the traffic we've registered going in and out of the region. I bet some of Garrand's guests went through Radbur on their way to the *Demeter*. That town's been a smuggler's paradise since the pashas were in power."

"So I'll—what—catch a ride with this Axmed?" Bolan said, looking at Brognola.

Spence clapped his hands together. "If you ask him nicely, yeah. And bring him a gift."

"I have a better plan," Bolan said bluntly. "You come with me and ask him yourself."

5

Gulf of Aden

Drenk stood in silence, his coat folded over his arms, as the mercenary called Yacoub showed him his cabin. "The drinks cabinet is full, of course, and the galley is stocked," he said, looking at his watch, then the floor. The mercenary wouldn't meet his eyes. Few men dared to, a thought that brought Drenk no end of amusement.

Drenk looked about and then said, "The others?"

The Moroccan twitched as if stabbed. "In—ah— in their own cabins."

"How many?"

"I don't see how that—"

Drenk cocked his head. He said nothing. Drenk was not one to repeat himself. Yacoub swallowed and said, "Three others."

"Is that all?" Drenk smiled. "How fortunate. I have always preferred intimate gatherings."

"We expected more, but no dice," Yacoub said, stepping toward the door. Drenk did not try and stop him, nor did he say anything about the way Yacoub's hand dipped for the gun on his hip.

"That is always the way, in these matters. Only the truly interested bother to show up," Drenk said without turning around. He heard the door shut behind him as the mercenary made a hasty exit, and he laughed.

Others had been scheduled to arrive. A dozen or more, in fact. He had taken care of three of them himself, waylaying them at airports and harbors. One he'd fed to the sharks in the Gulf. One he'd bribed. The third…well. That had been fun. For a moment, he allowed himself to enjoy the memory.

Then he turned back to the matter at hand. Only four. He'd seen Kravitz and the Arab as he boarded, but who was the fourth? The answer presented itself directly as the door to his cabin opened and a broad, craggy face peered in. "My drinks cabinet is full of African piss and French toilet water. What is in yours, half-breed?"

"Hello, Gribov," Drenk said, frowning slightly at the other man's rudeness. He knew Gribov, as men in their line often knew one another. Their paths had crossed over the years as they moved from employer to employer, selling their services to the highest bidder. Drenk knew dangerous men when he met them, and Gribov was a monster. Almost as bad as himself, though less…imaginative in some ways. Gribov killed like an animal, without care or consideration, and acquired scars for that reason.

"Are we friends now? Do we say hello to one another or write letters? Get out of my way," Gribov said, pushing past him to get to the drinks cabinet. "I'm surprised to see you. Your masters must want this boat very badly indeed."

Drenk shrugged. What his masters wanted or didn't want mattered little to him. He followed orders, as was his duty. "And who are you working for these days?" he asked. "Some Russian robber baron out to secure a new luxury craft?"

"The Yellow Chrysanthemum," Gribov grunted, turning away from the cabinet, a bottle of vodka in his hand. He smiled, showing steel-capped teeth. "As if it matters. One group of bastards is much the same as another, eh?"

Drenk ignored the taunt. "Only four of us," he said.

Gribov's smile widened and he held up a hand. "I got two. A man from the South American jungle and a Nigerian. He prayed to Allah as I peeled off his scalp." His smile faded as Drenk held up three fingers.

"That makes nine altogether, counting us. I wonder who got the others," he said. "The Arab, you think?"

Gribov snorted. "More likely the accountant. The Society is broken, but her soldiers are still about. Kravitz has more killers on his leash than he has legitimate accounts."

"So you say," Drenk said.

"So I know," Gribov replied. "One of them came for me, in Hong Kong, at the airport. Right in the toilet stall." He laughed. "I smashed his skull and finished my business as he lay twitching."

"Elegant," Drenk said. "Planning to confront Kravitz, then?"

"No. Better," Gribov said. "Planning to outbid him." He poked Drenk in the chest. "And you as well, half-breed."

Drenk resisted the urge to snatch the bottle from Gribov's hand and clout him with it. But there was no sense in starting a fight. Not yet.

Plenty of time for that later, he thought.

PIERPOINT SAT IN his cabin and stewed. He clenched his fists, imagining them wrapped around Garrand's thick neck. How had it all gone so wrong? The plan had been perfect. But Garrand's plan had been better, a treacherous part of him thought.

Pierpoint stood and began to stump about the cabin, his hands behind his back. He'd been played—he knew that now. He'd let his thirst for publicity blind him to the stupidity of the whole thing—of course it had been a trick.

Garrand was clever. That was part of the reason Pierpoint had hired him. He'd needed someone intelligent to oversee his security and to plan this operation. Garrand had known from the get-go what his job was, and he'd seemed fully committed, if not to Pierpoint, then to the money. Maybe that should have been the tip-off right there.

Pierpoint looked around the cabin, at the built-in bed and desk, at the nautical prints on the walls. Everything useful had been stripped when they'd stuck him in here. He was lucky they'd allowed him to keep his bootlaces. Not that he'd been planning to attempt an escape; what sort of publicity would that be, getting himself killed?

He was smarter than that, and Garrand knew it.

Stripping the room had simply been a precaution. Garrand always took precautions. Pierpoint stared blindly at the floor, wondering again where it had all gone wrong. The cynical part of him said it was the moment he'd decided to construct the *Demeter*. Getting in bed with the government had seemed risky at the time, but the potential benefits outweighed the costs. If the *Demeter* was a success, there was money to be made, and the environment could be improved.

He liked to imagine that sometime in the future— when Pierpoint Solutions was responsible for clean oceans, wind farms and hydroponic factories— they'd put up a statue of him, and it would say something like "The Man Who Saved the World." That wasn't too much to ask, was it?

The *Demeter* was supposed to be the first step on the road to that statue. On the road to a healthier world. And now it was going to be sold to the highest bidder, and the only statue Nicholas Alva Pierpoint was likely to get was a headstone.

He looked up as the door opened to admit one of Garrand's flunkies. The man stepped into the cabin holding a tray of food. He carefully pulled the door shut behind him, preventing Pierpoint any opportunity to slip past, even if he'd been so inclined.

"Yacoub," Pierpoint said. The man was one of Garrand's, but he'd always been sensible. He hadn't been enthused about the plan from the jump, Pierpoint recalled. He could use that. He'd always been good at finding the weak points and taking advantage of them.

"I brought food," Yacoub said, lifting the tray. "Fresh from the galley."

"And warmed in the microwave, no doubt, since the last I heard, most of the galley staff, other than Carmichael, are sitting on their hands in the hydroponics garden," Pierpoint said. "Where is Carmichael, by the way? I hope you haven't killed her. That woman earned me three Michelin stars. You can't replace quality like that."

"She's fine," Yacoub said, "down in the cove, where Sergei can keep an eye on her." He frowned as he said it. Pierpoint smiled grimly. That made sense. Carmichael had been a Royal Marine before she'd taken up cookery. Evidently Garrand had seen that Steven Seagal film, and he wanted to take no chances. Yacoub went on. "Besides, what do you have to complain about, anyway? You've got your own damn cabin," he said harshly.

"Of course I do. This is my ship, remember?"

Yacoub snorted. "Garrand might have something to say about that."

"And if not him, then those others you invited onboard certainly would, eh?" Pierpoint said softly. "Who are they, Yacoub? Who is he selling my *Demeter* to?"

Yacoub licked his lips. "Does it matter?"

"Humor me," Pierpoint said.

"If Garrand wants you to know, he'll tell you."

"Before or after he shoots me?"

"We're not shooting anybody. Not unless we have to," Yacoub said. But he didn't sound certain. "Do you want your food or not?" He held out the tray. Pierpoint hesitated. How far could he push the other man?

"Yacoub, I know you—you're a smart guy. Don't tell me you bought into this scheme of his," Pierpoint said, trying to widen the crack of unease he'd seen in the other man's eyes. "Surely you can see that he's in over his bloody head."

Yacoub looked at him. "Let's get one thing straight, Pierpoint—you don't know anything about me. And Garrand knows what he's doing." He dropped the tray of food on the desk. "Eat it, or don't."

Pierpoint watched him leave. Then, after a moment, he sat down to eat.

"How ARE OUR guests settling in?" Garrand asked as Yacoub came into the control room. "All packed away in their quarters without incident?" He kept his eyes on the radar, watching the numerous blips. Elements of the US 5th Fleet, among others, had set up a loose cordon in the Gulf. Ostensibly, they were part of the international task force combating piracy and trafficking, but Garrand knew he had their full attention at the moment.

"So far." Yacoub shuddered. "That bastard Drenk is a creepy one. And Gribov…"

"The less said about Gribov the better," Garrand admitted.

"I was hoping for more than four, though, the way you were talking, Georges," Yacoub said as he took a seat. He picked up an empty champagne bottle and eyed it critically. Whatever he was thinking, he didn't say anything, for which Garrand was grateful. "Will we get much of an auction?"

"Oh, we'll get plenty, I think," Garrand said, leaning back in his chair. "Those four men represent those who have access to roughly the equivalent of Germany's GDP." He doubted Yacoub knew what that was, but it sounded impressive.

"Well, we're going to need it when this harebrained scheme of yours winds up," Yacoub said. "Any thought on how we're getting out of here once we've gotten paid?"

"What makes you think we're leaving?"

Yacoub blinked. "What do you mean?"

"Whoever buys this tub is still going to need us until they can get a crew," Garrand said. "Delivery is part of the deal—a sweetening of the pot, if you will. We get this hulk moving, get it where it's supposed to go and drop off the hostages in the lifeboats or put them ashore in some godforsaken territory in dribs and drabs along the way. It keeps our opponents scrambling and off balance and keeps us safe." He pushed himself up. "Speaking of which, let's go check on the hostages."

Yacoub fell into step beside him. The hostages had been divided into easily manageable groups, one per deck. They were moved around every two hours, and the groups were swapped out as well, to keep anyone from making plans. Not that any of the hostages had showed that sort of initiative. But better safe than sorry.

Garrand led Yacoub to the cabana, where the hostages who'd greeted Pierpoint's arrival with cheers still sat slumped, worn down by stress and heat. Chuckles was on guard duty, watching from the shade. The big American didn't seem terribly bothered by the heat. He nodded as Garrand drew close. "Evening, skipper," he said.

"Any problems?"

"With this bunch? We should be so lucky," Chuckles said dismissively. Garrand couldn't help but agree. Pierpoint's guests had lost their enthusiasm not long after the man himself had vanished into the bowels of the *Demeter*. Once Pierpoint had been safely stowed, Garrand had ordered all of the cell phones, cameras and other assorted devices confiscated. Their purpose had been served, and it was time to lock the ship down. To their credit, the hostages had sensed the change in their captors and hadn't kicked up much of a fuss.

Leaving Chuckles to his boredom, Garrand and Yacoub descended into the upper hydroponics garden, where a number of people sat in the sweltering humidity among the spherical, slowly rotating planters. Borjan was in charge down here. The Serbian looked as uncomfortable as the people he was watching.

When he saw Garrand, Borjan grunted a greeting. One of the hostages, a member of the *Demeter*'s crew, had a bruise purpling on his face. Garrand looked at Borjan, who shrugged. "I warned him," the Serbian said.

"I'm sure you did. All the same, try not to kill any of them, please," Garrand cautioned, "especially the crew. We're going to need them if things go well." He looked around, taking in the garden. It was nothing but green and silver, lit by tubes that carried a soft glow. The air was thick with damp and the smell of growing things.

"And if they don't?" Borjan asked.

"They will," Garrand said firmly. Borjan subsided. He was speaking for the others, Garrand suspected. He glanced at Yacoub, who shrugged slightly. They were not patient men, by and large, though they were familiar enough with how he worked to fake it. But only for a while. Soon enough, they'd start to wonder where their money was and how they were going to enjoy it if they were still stuck on the *Demeter*.

They left Borjan staring after them and went to check on the group in the artificial cove, where Sergei was in charge. The former security man was sitting in the control cabin, his weapon across his knees, an unlit cigarette dangling from his lips. He perked up as Garrand knocked on the door. "Any trouble from the locals?" Garrand asked.

"None so far. Had a few boats out there sniffing around, but no one has gotten close," Sergei said, making to stand. Garrand waved him back to his seat.

"Real pirates. Probably wondering why we're sitting here, if they don't already know." Garrand looked toward the open section of the hull and the ocean beyond. The *Demeter* was right smack-dab in the middle of international waters, and no navy had the right to come after them. A few fishing boats were out there, however. Some of them would even be fishing. The rest would have been chartered by the media or by other interested parties. He scratched his chin, considering whether or not to send out another press release. *No,* he thought. One was enough for now. Let the international community dither a bit; the longer they wrangled over his demands, the longer he had to sell the *Demeter*.

He thought of the four men he'd welcomed aboard earlier. Gribov he'd met before—the big Slav was a nasty piece of work, despite his forced jocularity. He'd heard of the others, but knew little more than their names. He had no idea how they thought or how they might bid. Their employers had sent them armed with numbers and threats in equal measure, but it was only the former he was truly interested in.

"Maybe we should send a message," Sergei said, patting his weapon. "Let them know we're off limits."

"What, and start World War Three when we don't have to?" Yacoub asked.

"Better than sitting here." The two men looked at one another, not quite glaring, and Garrand recalled that they didn't particularly like each other. But they didn't have to be friends to get the job done.

"Patience is a virtue, Sergei," Garrand said, looking at the hostages, who were sitting by the edge. It would have been easy for any of them to simply slide into the water. None of them would, however. Sergei had taken the liberty of throwing chum in the artificial cove, attracting the attentions of dozens of sharks.

The Gulf of Aden was riddled with sharks, and between the pirates and the human trafficking that went on between Yemen and Somalia, the beasts had gotten a taste for human flesh. There were hundreds of them circling the *Demeter*, waiting for dinner. Garrand hoped they would be waiting for a while. He had no intention of feeding his hostages to the creatures—they were too valuable for that—but the unspoken threat was useful.

Garrand walked over and examined the group of hostages. Yacoub and Sergei followed close behind. "And how is everyone today, hmm?" he asked, his hands clasped behind his back. His face was still hidden behind his keffiyeh, but he had no doubt that they could understand him. He'd spoken in English. "Enjoying ourselves?"

Silence greeted his query. Eyes dulled by heat and fear looked at him. He recognized a number of the crew, including the head chef, Carmichael. She wasn't scared. Angry, and possibly wishing she had her hands on a butcher knife, but not scared. He smiled. "I'll take that as a yes. I know this isn't exactly the gala cruise your host promised, but we must all get along as best we can in these troubled times, no?" He gestured to the pale shapes sliding through the water in circles. "And if not, well, you can always see if their hospitality is any better, eh?"

"We should toss one in, just to show them what might happen," Sergei said, more loudly than was strictly necessary. Garrand shook his head.

"No, no, I think they grasp their situation clearly," he said. He moved back toward the control cabin and clapped a hand on Sergei's shoulder. "Thank you, Sergei." Then Garrand led Yacoub back to the upper decks, whistling as he walked.

"Pride goes before a fall," Yacoub said. "Carmichael looked like she wanted to gut you."

"She always looks like that. And so long as we sell this tub first, I think I'll survive." Garrand slapped a pipe. "Almost a hundred miles of pipe in this floating bucket. Nearly the same amount of maintenance tunnels, running along the interior of the hull. Did you know that?"

"No."

"Enough to kit out an entire town with a working

water system. All wasted, in a fool's dream," Garrand said. "How's Pierpoint getting on, by the by?"

"He's been cursing nonstop since we locked him into his cabin. Not a happy fellow, that one. Then, I suppose he has good reason."

"Hmm. Remind me to check on him later," Garrand murmured. He didn't feel guilty, exactly, but neither did he relish seeing the look in Pierpoint's eyes. He glanced back at Yacoub. "What's eating you? I know you have your problems with Sergei, but…"

"It's not Sergei," Yacoub said. "Well, not entirely." He stopped in the corridor. "I trust you, Georges, but this plan of yours…it's too complex. There are too many balls in the air, even for you. All it would take is one problem, just one, and this whole scheme will start to unravel."

"And that's why you're here, my friend. To make sure that no problems arise, yes?" Garrand said with forced heartiness. He clapped Yacoub on the shoulder and continued on. As he stepped out onto the deck, Garrand stretched and luxuriated in the feel of the ocean breeze. The sun was starting to slip below the horizon. The shore resembled a nest of newly stirred fireflies, and the distant ships were lit as bright or brighter.

"It is beautiful, is it not?" The voice was rough and rumbling. Garrand turned as Gribov ambled across the deck toward them, his hands stuffed into the pockets of his coat. "Lights on the water. Like the lanterns of the dead, shining up from beneath the Dnieper," the big man continued as he pulled out a packet of cigarettes, stuffed one between his lips and lit it.

"I'll take your word for that," Garrand said. "I trust your quarters are satisfactory?" He'd put his guests into the *Demeter*'s best cabins, though he doubted Gribov cared.

"It would be better with a woman," Gribov said. "Perhaps one of those trollops you are keeping below deck, eh?" He blew a plume of smoke into the air.

"They're hostages," Yacoub said. Gribov didn't look at him.

"Tell your monkey not to speak unless spoken to, Georges. Or I shall feed him to the sharks." Gribov smiled widely, displaying steel-capped teeth. Yacoub's eyes narrowed, but he said nothing.

"You're a guest here, Gribov. I'll thank you to refrain from feeding anyone, especially my second-in-command, to the sharks, without my express permission." Gribov frowned but didn't protest.

"If you cannot behave, maybe you should leave," Drenk said, as he joined the three men at the rail. Drenk was slim where Gribov was burly, but he nonetheless gave the impression of being muscular beneath his tailored suit. "Let the honored gentlemen of the Yellow Chrysanthemum send someone more professional to represent their interests in this matter." Drenk pulled a thin foil pack of gum out of his coat and popped a piece into his mouth. He chewed with relish, as Gribov's face flushed.

"You watch your mouth, you half-breed fool," the latter snarled.

"Gentlemen, please," Garrand said. "If we could save our sniping for tomorrow? I'm sure it'll make the bidding go all the quicker." He gestured toward the cabana. "Who wants a drink, eh?" Drenk and Gribov started for the cabana. Garrand hesitated when he saw Yacoub frowning. "Come have a drink, my friend."

"I hope you know what you're doing, Georges," Yacoub said.

"All part of the plan, my friend. All part of the plan."

6

Somaliland

Mack Bolan crouched against the rock wall, trying to
keep his head down. He could feel the rough surface
through the material of his fatigues. Bullets whined
through the air overhead, chewing chunks of mortar
and dust from the building behind him. He hefted the
UMP and finished popping home a new magazine
as bits of broken rubble pattered across his head and
shoulders. He'd already emptied one magazine on the
run. "Well, this is a fine mess you've gotten us into,
Spence," Bolan said.

The agent's plan had been fine, as far as the early
stages went. The insertion into the rocky hills and
gorges above the town of Radbur had come off without a hitch. They'd stowed the parachutes out of sight
and descended into the ancient town under cover of
night to meet Spence's contact. Only the minute
they'd reached the dusty streets, the dark had been

split open by the spastic light of gunfire and road flares. The town was seemingly under siege, though Bolan couldn't tell from what direction.

The air throbbed with the growl of vehicles and the shouts and screams of men. Someone had decided to conduct an early morning raid. It wasn't the local military, of that he was certain. From the glimpses he'd been able to catch of the aggressors, he thought they were Al-Shabaab militants. The flags they were flying—black with distinctive Arabic script—were a dead giveaway.

Normally Al-Shabaab confined their activity to southern Somalia. What they were doing here was anyone's guess. Bolan fired again, stitching a stone wall. Most of the closest militants had taken cover in a central building. The others were scattered throughout the town and were engaged in combat with the locals from the sound of things. That was just fine, as far as Bolan was concerned.

"This isn't my fault, Cooper," Spence growled, firing his own weapon over the wall. "It was your idea to parachute in." More shots came from the central building, peppering the street and the wall. The militants were persistent. Luckily, they were terrible shots, substituting quantity for quality.

"It was *your* plan for *me* to parachute in. I just made you come with me." Bolan was getting tired of being used to clean up agency messes while they sat at a safe distance. He hadn't started his war for their benefit and wasn't about to let them co-opt it for their own ends.

Spence cursed and hefted his weapon. He began to work the slide. "Jammed," he said.

"Covering," Bolan replied automatically. He rose and set the barrel of his weapon on the wall. The Executioner tracked a running shape and fired. The target went down like a sack of potatoes. The wall vibrated as it was struck again and again by the bullets of gunmen holed up in a nearby building. The wall looked as if it had lasted centuries, surviving weather and war, but a few more minutes of this and it would crumble. "We need a new plan," he said, looking toward the building where the majority of the fire was coming from.

"The plan is fine," Spence snapped. "It *was* fine until you had to start making changes. I shouldn't even be here! I'm not a goddamn field agent!"

Bolan didn't waste his breath arguing. Instead, he looked up. The sun was starting to rise. Once they lost the dark, they'd also lose the only real protection they had. The militants would realize they were facing only two men, and they'd swarm them. Bolan and Spence had to take the fight to the enemy.

Bolan popped a smoke canister free from his harness and pulled the pin. He lobbed the grenade over the wall and immediately grabbed for another. "Get ready to move," he said as he sent the second spinning along the narrow street. Colored smoke started spitting into the night air.

"Move where?" Spence demanded.

"Where do you think?" Bolan asked, pointing toward the building. "You said we needed to bring a gift, right? Well how about we give them the best gift of all—dead enemies."

"Enemy of my enemy is my friend, huh, Cooper?"

Spence said in a tone that might have been admiration. He grinned. "I can dig it."

"Then on your feet," Bolan said, freeing a third smoke grenade from his combat harness. He hurled it toward the building as he vaulted over the wall. Smoke flooded the street, caught in the grip of the sea breeze. He and Spence moved forward quickly, firing as they went. They took up positions on either side of the doorway. The smoke was blowing toward them and into the open building. The gunfire had slackened, and Bolan could hear coughing and cursing within.

He caught Spence's attention with a sharp wave. Spence nodded, and Bolan swung back from the door and drove his boot into it. Old hinges, ill-treated by time and the environment, popped loose of the wooden frame with a squeal, and the door toppled inward. Bolan was moving forward even as it fell, his weapon spitting fire. He raked the room beyond, pivoting smoothly, his UMP held at waist height. The gunmen screamed and died.

Bolan stalked forward like Death personified, his gun roaring. He heard Spence follow him inside but didn't turn. Despite his earlier complaints, the CIA agent was capable enough. Bolan pressed himself to a wall and sprayed the next room. The smoke was clearing, and he could see men moving, trying to find cover. They hadn't been expecting a direct assault. People rarely did. He took advantage of their disarray and palmed a grenade—not smoke, this time—off of his rig. He hooked the pin with his thumb and pulled it loose before rolling the grenade into the room beyond.

The explosion rocked the building. Dirt and dust

sifted down from above. He counted to three and stepped around the corner, weapon at the ready. Bodies greeted him, twisted and torn by the force of the explosion.

Bolan advanced slowly. He heard Spence enter the room behind him. The other man whistled. "When you kick in the door, you really kick in the damn door, Cooper." Bolan didn't reply. He scanned the bodies, checking for any signs of life. None appeared forthcoming, for which he felt no small sense of relief. His gamble had paid off, as he'd hoped it would. Spence, behind him, said, "Al-Shabaab, looks like. What are they doing this far north?"

"Maybe they heard there was a boat for sale," Bolan said.

"Hardy har har," Spence replied. He shook his head. "God, I hope not. We've got one terrorist group in the mix. We don't need another. This whole situation is already too complicated." He stepped past Bolan, treading on the dead with little concern.

And whose fault is that? Bolan thought. He heard the wet slap of bloody flesh striking the dirt floor and turned. One of the bodies had rolled over, and a man was gripping a pistol in one bloody hand. A white grin, fierce and unpleasant, split the militant's black beard, and Bolan began to raise his weapon, knowing as he did so that he wouldn't get a shot off in time.

He felt no fear, only frustration. To die here, like this, was unworthy. But was there really such a thing as a worthy death for a man like him? Or was there simply cessation, an abrupt end to a seemingly eternal war? The thought expanded, filling his mind in the microseconds before the militant fired.

"Cooper!" Suddenly, Spence was there, knocking him aside. Bolan stumbled. He heard the pistol boom. He saw Spence spin away, trailing red. Then he was on one knee and his UMP was firing. The militant pitched backward, arms flying out. He made no sound as he died, other than a soft exhalation. Bolan rose and turned. Spence lay on the floor, unmoving. Bolan moved quickly to his side.

"Spence."

The agent cracked an eyelid. "Did you get the license plate of that truck that hit me?" he wheezed. He touched his side and groaned. "Oh Jesus, I've been shot."

"That does tend to happen," Bolan said. He drew his combat knife and carefully slit Spence's shirt. Then he opened one of the two first aid packs he carried and dressed Spence's wound, after checking that the bullet wasn't lodged inside. The bullet had torn a ragged gouge in the side of Spence's chest, but his ribs appeared to be intact. It didn't look as if it had clipped anything important, besides flesh, but he didn't think the other man was going to be fit for duty anytime soon. "It's through and through. You won't be doing calisthenics for a while, but you're not going to bleed to death."

"That's a relief."

"Thank you," Bolan said.

"For what? I was just protecting an asset."

Someone shouted from outside. The sounds of gunfire had faded, but Bolan knew that one wrong move would see it start back up. "Sounds like someone is asking us what the hell is going on," he said as he helped Spence sit up.

"That'll be—ah!—Axmed and his boys, unless I miss my guess." Spence pressed his hand to his side and grunted in pain. "That's going to leave a mark."

"I've had worse," Bolan said, checking the wound. Before he could elaborate, there was more shouting from outside.

"Look, let me do the talking," Spence said from between clenched teeth. He glanced at Bolan. "Unless you speak Somali?" he asked hopefully.

"No," Bolan said. Which was true, as far as it went. Bolan knew a number of languages, and of those, one or two well. He could make himself understood in Arabic, which was spoken in Somalia, alongside English and Bravanese. But northern Somalis spoke a dialect Bolan was only somewhat familiar with.

"Great. Then keep quiet and get me outside." Bolan slid the other man's arm over his shoulder and pulled him to his feet, eliciting a stifled groan. Privately, Bolan had to admit that the CIA agent was tougher than he'd thought. Spence in one arm, and his UMP in the other, he hauled the agent to the door and kicked it open to reveal a semicircle of waiting assault rifles.

Spence said something in rapid-fire Somali, speaking as if he were afraid of passing out. For his part, Bolan kept his own weapon not quite pointed in the general direction of the ground. After a moment, a heavyset man stepped forward. He wore a ratty polo shirt and khaki pants and had a bandolier of ammunition pouches slung over his wide chest. He smiled, showing off a mouth of missing teeth. "Well, well, well…if it isn't my good friend Spence. Hello," he said in accented English.

"Good to see you, Axmed." Spence coughed.

"It is, I am sure." Axmed grinned and pulled an old-fashioned revolver—Belgian-made, Bolan thought—out of the holster beneath one thick arm. He cocked the revolver and aimed it at Bolan. "Now, how about you give me one good reason not to put a bullet in your treacherous skull, eh?"

7

"You want a reason? Fine, I'll give you a reason. You won't shoot me because then my friend here would stitch you up faster than your buddies can blink," Spence said hoarsely. "Cooper, meet Axmed, smuggler, pirate and asshole." He gestured with a bloody hand.

Axmed inclined his head in Bolan's direction but didn't lower his weapon. Neither did his men. Bolan examined them surreptitiously—they were a motley crew, apparently better fed than most Somali pirates, who were, in the end, often just fishermen pushed to desperation. These men were tough, armed and reasonably disciplined. This Axmed appeared to be a professional, as far as that went.

"You wound me, Spence. What have I done to deserve such hostility?" Axmed asked. The Somali had a deep voice, like a bell tolling up from cavernous depths.

"Well, you pointed a gun at us when we came all

this way to help you get rich," Spence said. He shuddered in Bolan's grip and touched his chest. "And at cost, I might add," he wheezed.

Axmed grunted. "Rich, you say?"

"Wealth of the high seas," Spence said.

"I'd think a pirate like you would be interested in that sort of thing," Bolan added.

Axmed looked at Bolan. "I don't know you. Spence called you Cooper, but I doubt that is your name... any more than 'Spence' is his."

"What's in a name?" Bolan said with a hard grin.

"Only devils and wizards hide their true names," Axmed said. "Or so my grandmother was fond of saying." He smiled and holstered his weapon. "Then, what did that foolish old woman know?"

"I guess you forgive me, then?" Spence asked.

Axmed stroked his chin. "If I were truly holding a grudge, I would shoot you in the face now and leave your body for the dogs. But that would be a waste of a bullet and against the laws of hospitality." His eyes flickered to Bolan. "Besides which, you and your friend here saved us the trouble of rousting these squatters..." He gestured to the dead militants. "Parasites, the lot of them. Seeking to usurp that which is not theirs. We've been wasting ammunition on them all night." He shook his head. "You said something about money?"

"I need someplace to sit down first, and a drink, if you're not feeling too religious," Spence said. Axmed indicated a good spot, and Bolan hauled the CIA agent there and helped him sit down. Someone brought over a bottle of something that smelled alcoholic, and Bolan passed it to Spence, who took it gratefully. "What's a pirate without grog, huh, Cooper?" he said.

"Marginally healthier than one with it. At least, that's what I'd guess from the smell," Bolan said as he looked around. Axmed met his gaze and grinned. He tapped the side of his nose.

"Allah will forgive us a bit of fortifying tonic, or so my grandmother always said." He kicked Spence's foot, and the agent winced. "Money, Spence. You still owe me from last time."

"And you owe me from the time before that." Spence coughed as he set the bottle aside. "Just like you'll owe me for this. Know that big boat just sitting out there in the Gulf?"

Axmed made a face. "I know it and have already decided against it. It's a fortress, and its new keepers are decidedly unfriendly." He gestured to the dead militants. "These southern dogs were planning to make a run at it, I'd wager—they wanted the town— *my* town—as a staging area. Though what they'd do with a ship like that, I don't know. They can barely drive those rattletrap jeeps they steal, let alone sail a vessel of that size." His men laughed, as if all too familiar with the inadequacies of the dead men. Axmed swiped the air with a hand. "No, that ship is not for the taking, I think."

"I can take it," Bolan said.

Axmed looked at him and then Spence. "Is he mad? Or just boastful?"

"Both," Spence said as he took another drink. "But he's not a liar, and that's the important thing. Cooper here can get you on that boat, sure as sin."

"And why would he do that?" Axmed peered at Bolan in suspicion. "What's in it for you, eh?"

"Maybe I'm just the charitable sort," Bolan said. Axmed snorted.

"You? Maybe. Spence? Never." He scratched his chin. "No, you are up to something, my friends. That is the only reason a man like Spence helps anyone. All his gifts have a hidden sting, and I would need to know the price of this one before I accept it."

Spence opened his mouth to reply, but Bolan cut him off. "There's no trick. You can have what you can carry."

"And what would I do with a ship that size? I am a humble fisherman," Axmed said.

"Who said anything about the ship?" Bolan asked. "I said you can have what you can carry." Axmed frowned, and his men stirred. Bolan wondered how many of them spoke English. Then he wondered whether it mattered.

"And the ship?" the pirate asked.

Bolan smiled.

Axmed looked at Spence, who shrugged and took another pull from the bottle. "You were right, Spence. He's a lunatic and a boastful one." The Somali looked at Bolan and gestured. "So…the deal, then, is what? You get us on the ship, we loot it and then you scuttle it?"

"Actually, I'll be scuttling it *while* you loot," Bolan said. "And freeing the hostages as well, though if you wanted to give me a hand in that regard, I wouldn't say no…"

Axmed laughed. "Ha! You do not ask for much, do you?"

"I ask for nothing at all. I'm giving you everything you might want," Bolan said.

As he'd expected, Axmed sniffed derisively. "You are asking us to be a distraction," he said bluntly. He wagged a finger at Spence. "I know your tricks. We are—what is the phrase?—running interference, yes? We will fight and die, like pirates, shedding our blood for your cause, blinded by greed."

Spence shifted uncomfortably and glanced at Bolan. "That…was the plan, yeah," he said. "That boat is worth a lot, Axmed. Hell, the parts are worth more than the whole—"

"I suspect to the right person, yes, but there are precious few of those about these days," Axmed said softly. "I am not deaf, dumb or blind, my friend. I know what is on that boat and what it is worth. And I know it's worth nothing to me."

"But—" Spence began, jerking upright. He groaned and clutched his side. Bolan made to kneel, but Axmed waved a hand and several rifles swung about to aim at the Executioner.

"It is worth nothing to me, Spence," Axmed said again. "But maybe you are worth something to those men in possession of it, yes? How much would they pay, those white men dressed as black men, for you and Cooper here?"

"They'd pay in lead," Bolan said.

"Very poetic," Axmed replied. "And maybe you are right. Or maybe you are wrong. Who can say, until the die is cast?"

"By the same token, who are you to say that ship is worth nothing to you until you walk its decks?" Bolan countered. He spread his hands. "Besides which, there are the hostages, who are all rich, and the ransom money."

"Ransom?" Axmed said. His men stirred. Bolan guessed they knew that word at least. Somali pirates found most of their funding through ransom demands.

"Several million at least," Bolan said. "I guess you don't know everything."

Axmed fondled the pistol holstered under his arm, tapping it briskly. "It seems not." He frowned and looked around. His men were speaking among themselves in quiet voices. Axmed chewed his bottom lip for a moment and then said, "How do I know you can get us onboard that ship?"

"How do I know you can get me to the ship?" Bolan asked.

Axmed sniffed. "I have boats. But do you have the ability to lead an assault? Are you any sort of fighter or just another of Spence's limp pets?"

"Hey!" Spence said weakly.

Bolan saw at once what Axmed was implying. He grinned mirthlessly and set his weapon down, as if unconcerned by the guns aimed at him. "Would you like a copy of my résumé?"

"A simple demonstration will do, I think." Axmed waved a hand, and two of his men stepped forward, handing their weapons to their fellows. They were big men, well-fed like the others, and built tough. They were also hardened fighters, and they weren't planning to play fair, to judge by their wide grins. It was a stalling tactic, Bolan suspected. Axmed was trying to figure out the angles, and he needed time to think. Bolan saw no reason to give him any more time than he'd already had.

He smoothly slid forward as the two men closed in on him. A fist whipped out, fast and heavy. Bolan tilted his shoulders, easily avoiding the blow. As it passed him, he drove both palms up into the exposed elbow joint and was rewarded with the snap-crackle-pop of breaking bone. The wounded man howled and staggered. Bolan caught the back of his shirt and hauled him forward as he shifted his weight to his left leg and drove his right knee up into the man's belly. Air exploded out of his opponent's lungs with a great whoosh, and Bolan gave him a shove, sending him to the ground.

The Executioner pivoted, snake quick, and swatted aside the second man's fist. A knife flashed, nearly opening a gash in Bolan's stomach, but he jerked back just in time. His second opponent had decided to stop playing around. Bolan ignored the knife and watched its wielder's eyes. It would have been a simple matter to draw his own, but he suspected it would be regarded as cheating by Axmed and his crew. Instead, he snapped forward, ducking beneath a wild slash to tackle his foe. As they slammed to the ground, Bolan caught the man's skull and bounced his head off the ground once, twice, three times, hard enough to ring his bells but not hard enough to crack his skull. As his opponent flailed about, dazed, Bolan drove a hard right across his jaw and knocked him out.

Bolan kicked the knife from the man's limp fingers and stood. Axmed smiled slowly and began to laugh. "Well, I am convinced." He clapped Bolan on the shoulder. "Now, what was that about a ransom?"

8

The Gulf of Aden

Garrand sat at the head of the table that dominated the *Demeter*'s stateroom. The room was tastefully decorated in polished wood and nautical memorabilia, including a few oil paintings of famous boats riding along storm-tossed seas.

It had taken them a day longer than he'd expected to get to this point. Kravitz had initially refused to meet with the others, as had Walid. Gribov and Drenk had almost come to blows twice. Threats had been exchanged and re-exchanged. Not to mention that his own men were growing restless, thanks to the delays. He could see them wondering if he'd lost control of the situation, if they should throw in with one of the money men. He'd expected this, of course. One didn't work with mercenaries for as long as Garrand had without understanding how they thought.

Treachery, like taxes, was inevitable. The question wasn't if, but when. Someone would lose faith in the plan and make a move—and that too was part of the plan. Garrand had factored it all in. But just because he knew it was coming didn't mean it didn't make him nervous.

Garrand let his attention shift back to his guests as he ran his fingers through the trickle of condensation that had slid from his bottle of beer to the tabletop. The four men, representatives of some of the largest cartels, organizations or consortiums, were talking at cross-purposes, making their bids clear. A lot of money was at stake, and they seemed to be under the impression that the *Demeter* would go to whoever spoke the loudest. He made strange shapes in the puddle of water to amuse himself while Kravitz droned on about why the bid of his current employers—whom he had yet to name—should be the winning one.

As offers went, it wasn't a bad one—a disgusting amount of money up front as well as stock in a number of profitable shell companies and the gratitude of some important wheelers and dealers on the European scene. Very tidy, very profitable, especially if he were intending to continue in his chosen career.

The problem was, the fussy little man had a voice like a wasp trapped in a tin can, too sharp and rhythmic to be fully ignored but too droning to fasten on to. Dressed nattily in something straight from Gieves & Hawkes of London, Kravitz looked every inch the highly paid accountant he claimed to be. Garrand let his eyes drift from Kravitz's stiff, thin features to the bulge beneath the man's coat. His tailor, whoever he was, had done an admirable job of hiding the shoulder holster, but if you knew what you were looking for, it was easy enough to spot. Garrand judged the weapon to be small caliber, probably French, maybe German. He wondered whether Kravitz had ever used it.

Walid Nur-al Din had certainly used the big bore revolver he carried on his hip. The representative of the Black Mountain Caliphate was a hardened guerrilla fighter and had waged jihad in more places than Syria. Like Gribov, he was a gun-for-hire, but Walid only worked for the Faithful. Walid was dark, broad and expressive. He wasn't as good at hiding his disdain for Kravitz as the others seated at the table.

The Syrian pounded a fist on the table, rattling the drinks. "Enough! Shut up, you puling ewe," he bellowed. Kravitz goggled at him but only for a moment. Then his watery eyes turned to ice and his hand twitched toward the holster beneath his arm. Garrand perked up, wondering if he would have to call for help.

"It is my turn to speak," Kravitz hissed. "*Robert's Rules of Order* clearly states—"

"Piss on Robert and his rules," Walid said. He thrust himself forward over the table. "And piss on you too, Kravitz. What do those old men you serve need with this vessel, eh? Do they not have enough castles? Do they need a floating one, as well? This ship is too valuable to deliver into the claws of wizened mummies… It belongs to those with the will to put it to good use!"

"And what would that be, Walid?" Drenk purred. "A floating opium den, perhaps? Or maybe a high-seas mosque?" Drenk upended his beer and finished it off. "You think too small."

"And you think big, is that it, half-breed?" Gribov rumbled, cracking his knuckles idly. "I wondered what that smell was."

"I was under the impression that it was you," Kravitz said as he took his seat. Before Gribov could retort, the little man gestured. "I have made my case, despite interruptions. Someone else may go, if they wish."

"Very orderly," Drenk murmured. He met Garrand's amused gaze and the corners of his lips twitched. Garrand's eyes widened as Drenk named a figure and then continued, "That is what the Black Serpent Society is offering, Monsieur Garrand. And not a penny more."

Hiding his astonishment behind a sip of beer, Garrand swallowed and said, "Forgive my impertinence, Mr. Drenk, but you do not appear to understand how an auction works." *Then, for that much money, maybe you don't need to,* he thought.

"I know how auctions work, but this is not an auction, is it?" Drenk said, lifting his empty bottle and giving it a shake. "Auctions are legal. No, you are looking for a fence, Monsieur, not a buyer. You are looking for someone to take this albatross off your hands, so you might disappear back into the hinterlands of mercenary work as quickly as possible." Drenk paused and smirked. "Or, perhaps you're looking to retire… Either way, this is not an auction." He set the bottle down and leaned back, his hands clasped behind his head. "So, it is for you to choose the best price for your ill-gotten gains. Not for us to bid against one another."

"He's right," Gribov said, knocking on the table with his knuckles. "We are the only four to show up

to this little...party of yours. We are your only potential buyers."

"And be assured that I am grateful," Garrand said.
"That does not change the fact that I am in control
of this vessel. Definitions aside, money talks. I have
heard two offers—what of the others?"

Gribov grunted and motioned to Walid. "After
you," he said sullenly. Walid sniffed and set his hands
down on the table. Before he could speak, however,
Yacoub burst into the stateroom. Garrand spun.

"What is it?" he snapped.

Yacoub frowned. "Ships," he said. Garrand cursed
and stood. He looked at his guests and smiled apolo-
getically.

"Gentlemen, if you'll excuse me." He hurried after
Yacoub without waiting for a reply. "What ships?"
he hissed as the door to the stateroom swung shut.

"Those ships," Yacoub said, pointing through the
closest porthole. Garrand saw a number of vessels
in the distance, of all sizes and bearing the flags of
many nations. The Maritime Security Patrol had gotten reinforcements, it seemed. Not unexpected, but
worrying nonetheless. Garrand's scheme hinged on
the *Demeter* resting in international waters, outside
of any particular jurisdiction, thus necessitating com-
munication between the various interested parties
and governments. Bureaucratic conversations were
measured in days, rather than minutes. But if they
were massing...

He shook his head. "How many?"

"No clue," Yacoub said. "More than I like. Planes,
too. The radar sounds like a techno-rave concert."
Garrand had left two men in the control room at all

times to monitor radio traffic and the radar. They had orders to alert him or Yacoub if something happened, and he allowed himself a small moment of satisfaction at his foresight. Yacoub stopped and turned. "Tell me this was part of your plan."

Garrand held up his hands. "Of course it was. What sort of fool do you take me for?" he asked as images of an international task force swarming the decks filled his head before he shook them aside. That, too, had been prepared for. He had boats and Jet Skis in the cove—all manner of vehicles to enable a select few to escape. "That's why we still have the hostages."

"The hostages won't matter if they decide to retake the boat, Georges," Yacoub said. "We don't have enough firepower to see them off if that happens."

"No, but we have enough to make them think long and hard about it," Garrand said. "We have a surplus of time, Yacoub. It'll be days before the Maritime Patrol gets the okay to launch a strike. By that time, we'll be sailing for safer waters and feeding them hostages to keep them off our backs." He said it with as much confidence as he could muster and was rewarded with a terse nod.

Yacoub had been a loyal right hand for years; Garrand wasn't sentimental, but it frustrated him to see doubt in the other man's eyes. Yacoub was the only one he could count on when it came down to it. Garrand sighed and took Yacoub by the shoulders. "The plan still holds, my friend. We are simply buying time. In a few hours we will have our buyer, and we will set sail. By the time they start pursuit, we will be off this ship and safely away, rich as Croesus and without a care in the world. They haven't seen our faces, and while I do not doubt that someone, somewhere, suspects something is going on, they are not here."

He smiled. "The *Demeter* is unassailable and, by extension, so are we. So relax."

9

"A frontal assault, hey?" Axmed shouted over the roar of the motorboat's engine. "You are mad, aren't you?"

Mack Bolan, holding tight to the side of the boat, could only nod. He was in favor of the quick, lethal strike, but Axmed seemed to be working from a different playbook. The six motorboats were packed to the prows with desperate men—more of them, in fact, than Bolan had expected. He'd figured Axmed could muster two dozen men at most. Instead, he had almost twice that, and all of them armed with military surplus stolen from the Ethiopians and the Somalis. On another day, they might have been training those weapons on Bolan himself, but today they were his allies. At least for the moment.

Once he'd heard about the money, Axmed had been easy to convince. Even better, despite his earlier dismissal, the pirate was obviously still enamored of the idea of looting the super-yacht. He'd agreed to launch an assault, right under the eyes of the Maritime Patrol no less.

"We will not wait for you, of course," he'd said solicitously before they'd left Radbur. "You cannot expect that. While my men will fight like lions, lions are not known for hanging about where they can be easily shot, yes?"

Bolan hadn't argued. In truth, he hadn't expected anything more. The pirates were a distraction, and once they'd made enough noise, and caused enough trouble, they could leave. He didn't trust Axmed not to try to take the *Demeter* for himself. Although Bolan had no small amount of sympathy for fishermen driven to piracy in order to survive, Axmed was a career criminal and a born opportunist.

They'd waited for night to launch the attack. It was a smart play. Radbur sat between the Maritime Flotilla and the *Demeter*, so there was little chance of the pirates being intercepted. Nonetheless, the fewer eyes on them, the better. Bolan had conducted enough off-book operations to understand that a quick strike, before anyone on the ship or off realized what had happened, was for the best.

Plausible deniability, as Spence would have said, had he not been sitting back in the village, waiting for his people to retrieve him. With his wound, the CIA man would have only slowed Bolan down. Spence hadn't even bothered hiding his relief, though Bolan didn't have the heart to blame him.

Bolan gestured toward the *Demeter*. "Aim for the front of the hull," he said, pitching his voice to carry over the engines. "It worked for them, and it'll work for us."

"A lock once broken is never as secure, huh?" Axmed said.

"Something like that." Bolan glanced over the side of the boat and saw something gray sweep beneath the froth. A fin broke the surface momentarily before vanishing as the shark shot away, into the depths. Axmed chuckled.

"It seems we are not the only sharks in these waters," the pirate said. Bolan nodded and hefted his weapon. He'd been up close and personal with sharks more times than he cared to recall.

As the motorboats surged forward, Bolan let his mind drift, falling easily into that calm state that preceded battle. He knew he was living on borrowed time. He had been since the day he'd come home to find his family in ruins.

He had declared war against the underworld then. He had punched, shot, stabbed, burned and smashed his way through the ranks of the Mafia, the Yakuza and more. Hundreds had died by his hand over the years, sent on to their final judgment. And one day, his war would claim him as its final sacrifice.

He felt no fear at the thought of his inevitable death—only curiosity as to the form it would take. Would it be a bullet in the back, as quick as the snuffing of a candle's flame? Or something more torturous, like fingers around his throat or a knife in his guts?

Either way, the Executioner would meet his end without fear or hesitation. *And hopefully, I'll take plenty of bad guys with me,* Bolan thought.

One of Axmed's men pointed and shouted something. Bolan snapped out of his reverie as the hull of the *Demeter* expanded, filling the horizon. It was bigger than he'd first thought.

"Like a chicken waiting to be plucked," Axmed said, slapping one of his men on the shoulder.

"Big chicken," Bolan replied.

Axmed laughed. "Bigger the chicken, the more she can feed," he said, spreading his arms. "And we will have guests to help us—look!" Bolan saw a number of boats hurrying toward them or on parallel courses.

"How many men do you have?" he asked.

"Not mine," Axmed said. "There are many villages on this coast, and all of them have men with boats. They have all heard about this ship. They see us, they think 'what do they know, that we do not?' and they follow, like dogs on the scent."

Bolan shook his head. "You think they'd know better."

"They do. But knowledge does not fill an empty belly or buy you what you need to live. It does not patch your boat or repair your nets. Knowledge, such as you understand it, is useless to men like them. Desperation drives them."

"But not you," Bolan said.

Axmed snorted. "No. Not me. I like what I do. I enjoy it most heartily, and I will do it until I die. Which may be today, unless you are as good at your job as Spence claims because they've spotted us." He crouched on the bottom of the boat, and Bolan peered over him to look at the *Demeter*. Flood lights had snapped on, washing the surface of the water in brightness. Sharks thrashed in the sudden glare, diving deeper to spare their eyes.

"I can almost smell all of that lovely money,"

Axmed said. He glanced at Bolan. "You're sure it's that much?"

"That's what I was told. Plus whatever else you can find." He pointed. "Upper decks will have the cabins, the galley and the party areas."

"Lots of wealthy hostages," Axmed said.

Bolan agreed. "But they're mine. If you so much as touch them, I might forget we're friends." He let an edge of menace creep into his words. "You wouldn't like that, Axmed."

"So Spence said," Axmed replied. "You really think you could take us all?"

There was no threat there, Bolan judged, merely curiosity. He nodded. "If I had to."

Axmed clapped him on the shoulder. "Ha! I like you. Spence is too tricky by half, but you're as solid as a brick. Straight ahead, full throttle."

"Thanks, I think," Bolan said. He checked his watch. "How long can you give me?"

"You mean how long will it take us to loot the ship?" Axmed scratched his chin. "It depends on how much resistance we face. If I were on the other side, I would consolidate my men at a few key areas and leave the rest of the ship to, well, us." He swept out a hand. "Too big to properly defend, you see."

"And you won't fight unless they cross you, is that it?" Bolan asked.

Axmed shrugged. "We are not soldiers, Cooper. We are thieves. We will take what we can get and flee. But there are more of us than there are of them, if Spence is to be believed, and they will be more concerned with you, if all goes well, so…who can say? Perhaps we will not flee all that quickly." He nudged the satchel on Bolan's back. "You will let us know before you scuttle her, I trust."

"Sure," Bolan said. "When you hear explosions, run." The satchel was packed with the tools of the saboteur's trade—C4, detonators and anything else Bolan could think to ask for. He had a rough idea of the best places to plant the explosives, but only after he'd gotten the hostages, including Pierpoint, to safety. The ship's schematics were unavailable, held under digital lock and key by Pierpoint Solutions— another reason Spence wanted Pierpoint safely off the boat. Bolan hoped the crew could point him to the weak points. Failing that, Pierpoint himself might be able to do so.

Bolan had passed out a supply of grenades, including fragmentation and smoke, to Axmed's men before they'd left Radbur, the "gifts" Spence had insisted that they bring. Then Bolan had trained the men on proper use and handling.

"Ah, there's our cue," Axmed said as one of the heavy searchlights mounted on the upper deck of the *Demeter* caught them. Bolan shaded his eyes and looked up, trying to gauge the height of the super-yacht. It wasn't as tall as it had been when it was a cargo vessel, but it was still taller than anything calling itself a yacht had the right to be.

"Don't stop," Bolan said. "No matter what, just keep going. If you stop or retreat, it's over, and we'll never get a second chance."

"Do not presume to tell me my business," Axmed said. He unholstered his pistol and cocked it. "I've been doing this since I was a boy splashing in the bilges of my father's boat." He turned and shouted something in his own language. The man at the tiller hunched forward, as if to encourage the motor boat to greater speed through sheer force of will.

A desultory fusillade from the deck, high above, greeted their approach. That had likely been enough to discourage similar attempts from other pirates, but not this time. Axmed's men fired back, though there was little chance of hitting anything. It was more in the way of defiance, the little man shouting at the big one, letting him know he's not intimidated.

The hull was still partially open where Garrand's people had made their entrance. Some attempt at preliminary repairs had been made, but there was still a gap large enough to fit the motor boats one at a time. Bolan held out his hand to one of the pirates, who clutched a battered rocket launcher to his scrawny chest. "Time to knock on the door," Bolan said. The man hesitated and looked at Axmed.

"Give it to him," Axmed said. "Let us see if he is everything Spence said he was."

Bolan hefted the rocket launcher and checked it over. It was old but still in working order. He whispered a silent prayer to the Universe that it wouldn't blow up in his hands and took aim. It wasn't easy, with the motor boat rocking beneath his feet, but he found his target and pulled the trigger.

10

"It'll be over by tonight, I expect." Yacoub set a bottle of Burgundy on the desk in Pierpoint's cabin. Pierpoint looked at him, trying to gauge the emotion he heard in the other man's voice. He hoped he was finally getting through to Garrand's second-in-command. He needed an edge if he were going to fix things.

"Oh? And who will it be, do you think? The barmy terrorist? The Aryan accountant? Or one of the two scary bastards? Or someone else I haven't heard about?" he asked as he sat up on the bed. He had showered but he hadn't shaved and his clothes felt grungy. "Garrand isn't in control of the situation. From what you've told me, these are some dangerous characters. More dangerous, I think, than your boss suspects."

"He knows what he's doing," Yacoub said stiffly. Was that a hint of doubt? Pierpoint didn't know, but he decided to act as if it were.

"Does he? Maybe so—but I think he's bitten off more than he can chew. How much of his plan has he shared with you or the others? Georges is a sneaky one. What if this is all a dodge? What if he's planning to run off with the money and leave you here holding the bag?"

Yacoub picked up the bottle of wine. "Maybe you've had enough," he said.

"Are you telling me you've never thought about it?"

Yacoub was silent. Pierpoint restrained the urge to smile. "I know you, Yacoub. You were a good employee. So was Georges, come to that. Otherwise, I wouldn't have asked him to do what he—what you—did. But that was my mistake. Yours is thinking that a guy who'd betray one person wouldn't do it to another."

Yacoub shook his head and set the bottle back down. "And if you're right…so what?" he said after a moment. "What can I do?"

"You can help me." Pierpoint stood. "Get me out of here. Help me get the others out." The hostages weren't quite an afterthought, but Pierpoint felt a twinge of guilt for not being more concerned. He knew Garrand wouldn't hurt them—if it was more profitable to keep them alive—but they were still Pierpoint's responsibility. He had invited them on this cruise to boost the *Demeter*'s profile. His guests and the crew were hostages because he'd chosen to trust the wrong man, and he was determined to fix that mistake before it got any worse. He had a reputation to maintain, after all.

Yacoub looked at him, startled. "What?"

"This is still my ship, Yacoub. I built her. I know every inch of her. And I know how to evacuate her. Help me, and I'll help you. I'll get you out from under this. Heck, I'll give you Georges's old job, if you want it."

Yacoub blinked. "I'll think about it." He backed toward the door, eyes narrowed. Pierpoint watched him go and said nothing. He wondered if he'd overplayed his hand. If he had, he would need to take other measures.

He knew every inch of the *Demeter*. He had overseen the installation of every piece of equipment, including the secondary control room where the pumps that could flood the lower decks with seawater were located. Once those pumps were activated, the *Demeter* would sink. And hopefully, it would take Garrand with it.

GRIBOV STABBED THE tabletop with his finger and growled out an amount. "And a third of that in raw opium, as well as other substances, should you wish," he added grudgingly.

Walid and Kravitz fumed silently. Gribov's bid had made their own look like so much chicken feed.

Garrand nodded, surprised by the amount. It was comparable to Drenk's offer, but with the addition of the drugs, it was possible it would come out to more after resale. He leaned back, considering. Then he looked at Walid. "From your face, I'd say you've been outbid."

Walid turned away with a muttered curse. He shoved himself to his feet and stalked across the room, fists clenched. The others laughed, save Kravitz, whose offer looked decidedly puny next to those of Drenk and Gribov. Garrand watched as Kravitz stood and followed the Syrian, face unreadable. *Wheels within wheels,* he thought. Depending on who Kravitz was working for, he might be willing to pool his funds with Walid's for a significant bid. There was still some fight left in them, he hoped. Enough to make things interesting.

Garrand glanced at Drenk, wondering whether his earlier words had been the truth or merely a stalling tactic. Gribov's pride wouldn't let him be outbid, but if Drenk were serious, that narrowed the field of potential buyers considerably.

He tapped the table, thinking.

He was still thinking when the radio clipped to his body armor shrilled, and Yacoub's voice said, "Trouble."

Garrand cursed and shot to his feet. "Where?"

"The cove. Get down here. Now." Garrand could hear the strain in his second-in-command's voice. *The cove,* he thought. Sergei. He'd hoped it would be Borjan, but Sergei was an obvious second choice. The Russian was impatient, vicious and too eager to solve his problems with a bullet.

Garrand looked at his guests. Drenk smiled at him. "Something we can help you with?" he said, his smile widening nastily. Garrand shook his head.

"No, thank you. Enjoy the wine and food while I handle what will surely be a minor personnel matter." He left quickly, hurrying down through the decks, grabbing men as he went. He had a feeling he would need them. His heart thumped in anticipation of the confrontation to come. He would have to be firm—

ruthless even. He couldn't afford to appear weak, not in front of the others. He had the situation well in hand, but they needed to be reminded of that.

When he reached the cove, Yacoub was waiting for him at the central bulkhead, gun in hand and a grim look on his face. "It's Sergei…" he began. Garrand waved him to silence.

"I know, I know."

"He took a shot at me. Was that part of your plan?" Yacoub asked nastily.

"Of course not." Garrand didn't look at him. "How's Pierpoint?"

"Why don't you visit him yourself and find out?"

"Now, now, is there any cause for that? I've been busy, and I doubt he wants to see me. It wasn't like we were friends," Garrand said with a shrug. Yacoub was being unusually snide. *Stress,* Garrand thought. That was it. Everyone was tense to breaking, except him. *Stick to the plan, Georges, and all will be well.* He took a deep breath.

"He's got the others riled up. We should have moved them around more," Yacoub said accusingly. "I know we were more worried about Borjan, but…"

"Can't be helped. Besides, Sergei has been getting on my nerves. Too quick to shoot, too slow to think. That's a problem that needs solving. Let's go see what he wants." Garrand handed his rifle to one of the others and stepped through the doorway. He walked along the gantry that led down to the artificial quay, his hands raised and extended.

Sergei was waiting for him below, one arm draped lazily over a woman's shoulders. She was one of the hostages, though Garrand couldn't remember her name. *Actress? Model? No...reality TV star.* Regardless, not very important, save in terms of social cachet. She looked decidedly nervous. Then, if Sergei had been nuzzling his neck, Garrand would have been worried, as well.

Sergei held a pistol in his other hand and was idly tapping it against his hip as he kissed the woman. Formerly in the Russian special forces, or so he claimed, Sergei was quick, quicker than Garrand, and a better shot. But he had all the wit of a brick.

Three other mercenaries were stationed with Sergei. None of them looked happy with the situation. *Sergei aired his grievance, and you went along, but now it's all getting a bit uncomfortable,* Garrand mused. Most of the security staff had thrown in with him, but that didn't mean they were entirely comfortable guarding prisoners they had, until recently, shared a mess hall with. Money went a long way toward easing that particular discomfort, but they hadn't seen any yet.

"I thought we talked about this, Sergei," Garrand called out as he walked along the gantry. "I asked you not to touch the hostages, didn't I?"

"You say a lot of things, Georges," Sergei replied, not looking at him. "Did I hit Yacoub?"

"No, but not for lack of trying," Yacoub shouted.

"Pity," Sergei said, smiling at Garrand. "I'm bored. I will have her. And maybe I'll feed a few of them to the sharks." He swung a hand out and indicated the water-filled section of the cove where every so often, a shark's fin broke the surface.

Garrand was about to reply when a sound caught his ears. Motors, and coming fast. That wasn't unusual. The local pirates had been circling for days. They were as bad as the sharks, in some ways, but less dangerous. The *Demeter* was simply too large for them to make an attempt, especially with the Maritime Patrol in close proximity.

"Pay attention, Georges," Sergei snapped.

"Sorry. I have a lot on my mind," Garrand said. "What do you want exactly?"

"I told you." Sergei kissed the woman's cheek, and she tried to squirm away. The other hostages stirred—most of them were crewmembers rather than passengers. Sergei's men swung their rifles up, and the hostages settled back. Garrand frowned. Things could get messy very quickly, unless he calmed Sergei down.

"Let her go, Sergei," Garrand said softly. "I told you... I want no one harmed. We start killing them, we'll lose our protection." He gestured toward the sea. "They're just waiting for us to give them an excuse, man. Think!"

"You told us it would be over in a day, maybe two," Sergei said, pulling the woman close. "It's been three days, Georges. Our window closed hours ago. We're surrounded by ships with no chance of escape, even if you do sell this stinking tub."

"Don't you think I planned for this? For all of it?" Garrand looked around, knowing that Sergei was only saying what most of his men were thinking. "I told you it might take more than a few days. And we are still in international waters, don't forget. We're surrounded, yes, but that's a relative term when it comes to the sea. And while we have them—" he pointed to the hostages "—no one will make a move. Unless someone does something stupid, like, say, kill one of the hostages. The plan requires…"

"Damn your plan and the horse it rode in on," Sergei roared.

Garrand stopped. "What? That doesn't even make sense, Sergei." As he spoke, he reached for the pistol holstered on his belt. If he could get it out, he might be able to intimidate Sergei into settling down. Garrand intended to shoot him as soon as possible, of course. But best to do it when the hostage was safely out of the way. As he took hold of the pistol, the sound of the motors was growing louder. He heard the rattle of gunfire but dismissed it. He had more important matters to attend to. "Now, let her go, and we can discuss your grievances at our leisure. I should mention that I was quite close to selling the *Demeter* until you interrupted—"

Sergei spat a curse in Russian. Before Garrand could reply, however, the cove shuddered as something exploded against the already ruptured hull, filling the air with smoke and fire. Garrand ducked aside and stared in disbelief as a motor boat shot through the smoke and skidded across the water toward him.

11

Axmed's motor boat was the first through the gap. It surfaced across the water, engine wailing, scattering the sharks that had gathered there. Bolan hunched and clung tight, waiting for his moment. Axmed stood in the prow and fired his pistol at nothing in particular, shouting out curses and oaths in equal measure. His men followed suit, yelling and firing as more boats skidded after them.

Garrand's men had started shooting as soon as the first boat appeared. But there weren't enough of them, and hitting a moving target was hard, even for trained gunmen. One or two of Axmed's men were plucked from their feet and sent sailing into the churning waters, but not enough.

Bolan peered at the artificial shoreline and saw a huddled group of people—weaponless, bedraggled. *Hostages,* he thought. There was no one else they could be. Not all of them, though. Not by a long shot. Going by the uniforms, some were crew. Garrand had

had inside help, but not everyone was in on it, apparently. That made Bolan feel a bit better about the odds. He raised his UMP and fired a quick burst at the men on the shore, hoping to send them running.

"Remember," he said, catching Axmed's eye, "Leave the hostages to me."

"Pah, what do I need with them when I have this whole lovely ship to plunder?" Axmed fired his pistol again, and then the prow of the motor boat struck the shallows of the artificial cove, grinding to a halt on the manmade reefs that kept the sharks at bay. Axmed was first out of the boat. Bolan and the others followed.

The Executioner moved quickly, firing as he ran. Quick, controlled bursts sent most of Garrand's men heading for cover. One, a large man holding a woman, gawped at the newcomers. Nevertheless, he swiftly leveled his weapon and shoved the woman aside. Bolan fired, plucking a gout of red from the man's skull and dropping him where he stood. Axmed's men moved around him, shouting and firing, as Bolan helped the woman to her feet. "Are you all right?" he asked, hauling her out of the line of fire. He pulled her behind an overturned motorboat. "Can you walk?"

"I—I think so," she said, her voice ragged.

"Where are the other hostages—do you know?" He caught her chin, turning her face toward him as a gun rattled somewhere nearby. The other pirates were reaching the cove now, and many of Axmed's men were spilling up the shore toward the gantry and the bulkheads beyond. Others lay dead, either in the water or on the shore. Garrand's men had been caught by surprise, but they were still professionals. "Don't look at that…look at me," he said. She was panting, beginning to hyperventilate—a not uncommon reaction to having a gun shoved in one's face. Bolan spoke calmly, forcing himself to slow down despite the adrenaline surging through him.

"Take deep breaths," he said, trying to distract her from the firefight going on around them. "I need you to focus—where are the others? Do you know?"

"The-they're a-all over—they split us up—t-three groups, I think," she rattled, eyes wide. She was on the verge of shock, he suspected, but holding on by her fingernails. "The place with the plants…"

"Hydroponics," Bolan said. "And?"

"The—the deck." She closed her eyes. "They've got Nicky somewhere, too, but I don't know where." Bolan realized she was talking about Pierpoint. Before he could ask her to clarify, someone joined them.

"His cabin. B deck," the woman said. "I heard them talking about it earlier." She extended her hand over the quietly sobbing woman's shoulder. "Carmichael, galley crew."

"Cooper," he said automatically as he shook her hand. "U.S. Justice Department."

Carmichael's eyes widened. "Bit out of your jurisdiction, aren't you?"

"What's a jurisdiction?" Bolan asked with a grin. Her hand was hard and rough, and her accent was Estuary English. Posh, without the slurred edge of the upper classes. "Galley…you're the cook?"

"Chef, actually." Carmichael peered over the top of the boat. "Oh good, you shot Sergei. Never liked him. Told me my soufflé was flat, the dodgy bastard."

"Glad to be of assistance," Bolan murmured. "Where's B deck?"

Carmichael pointed up. "One from the top. Pierpoint had a cabin up there. 1-A, I think. Biggest one, of course. Down the hall from the stateroom."

"Of course," Bolan said.

Carmichael caught his tone. She smiled wryly. "He ain't that bad. Arrogant, conceited, but…good pay, good working conditions. Good benefits, too." She ducked as a bullet caromed off the boat.

"I'm here to save him, not give him my résumé," Bolan said. "Let's get back to the others." The Executioner hurried them to the rest of the hostages, who had taken cover nearby, and started gesturing toward the control station at the top of the shore. "Can anyone operate those controls if I can clear them?" he shouted. "Anyone?" One man, dressed in a bedraggled crew uniform, nodded and made to speak. Bolan didn't wait. He had to get them out of the line of fire as quickly as possible. "Good. We need to lock this area down after our friends there have made their exit, do you understand?"

"By friends you mean the pirates?" Carmichael asked.

"The enemy of my enemy is my friend," Bolan said.

"And after we lock it down, what then? Just sit here?" one of the other crewmen demanded. "I'm not a fan of that."

"Neither am I," Bolan said, "but we have to work with what we've got. If I can rescue the others, I'll bring them back down here." He cast a quick glance over the motor boats lined up on the shore. "Are all of these ready to go?"

"I checked them myself, before…all of this," another crewman said. His nametag read Annandale. "They're all gassed up and ready to go, if we can get them in the water without getting our heads blown off."

"Good. That's our way out. Can anyone use a gun?"

"We all can," Carmichael said, indicating the crewmembers. "I was in the territorial army. Stevens there was a squaddie, and the others have all served." She grinned at Bolan's expression. "Pierpoint isn't stupid, Mr. Cooper. This cruise was a stunt, sure, but we're not bloody idiots, no matter what you might have thought." She peered toward the ongoing gunfight and frowned. "Then, I never figured we'd have a bloody war to contend with."

"War is always something that happens to other people," Bolan said. He checked his UMP and took a breath. "Right, time to clear some space. Keep your heads down." As he stood, his keen gaze swept the impromptu battlefield, taking in as much detail as he could at a glance. The cove was large enough that the fight had moved steadily upward. Garrand's mercenaries were positioned near the central bulkhead—the main artery of the ship. The remaining pirates were mostly clustered around the other two bulkheads, trying to reach them to get into the ship proper. A small group of mercenaries had holed up in and around the control station. Those were his targets.

He plucked one of the M84 stun grenades dangling from his combat harness and, after he'd popped the pin, sent the canister sailing toward the small group. The grenade emitted a loud bang of 180 decibels along with a flash that could cause temporary blindness, deafness and ringing in the ears. Bolan kept his eyes shut as the grenade went off. From the yells, some of Axmed's men hadn't followed suit, despite his earlier warnings.

Bolan swept the barrel of his UMP across the gantry. A man fell, jitterbugging in his death throes, his weapon chattering as his fingers tightened convulsively around the trigger. *That's two,* Bolan thought as he climbed over the hull, his UMP spitting. Garrand's men fell back in good order, streaming toward the main entry, as he'd hoped.

Axmed and his men had split into smaller groups. Those who had survived the assault were already moving toward the undefended doorways, avoiding the knot of defensive fire erupting from Garrand's men. Axmed caught Bolan's eye just before he ducked through a doorway, and he grinned. The pirate was taking advantage of the confusion to slip away. *Fair enough,* Bolan thought. He hadn't expected Axmed to stick around for the heavy lifting, after all. As long as enough of his men were still around to keep the enemy's attentions divided, that was fine by him.

Bolan advanced on Garrand and his men, firing as he moved. When he emptied the clip, he ejected it and smoothly reloaded without taking his eyes off the enemy. He spotted Garrand, identifying the mercenary from his photo, where he stood, shooting at Axmed's men. Garrand turned as Bolan reached the gantry rail and shouted an order. Guns turned on Bolan and he was forced to lie flat and fire through the railing at the mercenaries.

He emptied another magazine and reloaded as bullets spanged off the railing all around him. Chips of metal bit into his cheek and he cursed as he rolled away, slamming the new magazine home. Still on his back, he fired blind. The soldier was rewarded with another scream and, then, a moment of silence. He got to his feet and caught hold of the railing, swinging himself over. The central doorway was empty save a few bodies. Bolan hunkered next to the aperture and sent another grenade into the corridor beyond. Then he motioned for Carmichael and the others to make a run for the control station as he hauled the door closed.

It slammed shut and he spun the locking mechanism, sealing it. He saw Carmichael and the others doing the same, shutting the other two doors and locking them. Bolan looked back at the control station and saw another crewman inside, his hands running across the controls. Whether he could keep the doors sealed from inside or not, Bolan didn't know, but for all their sakes, he hoped so.

Bolan rejoined the group. "Think you can hold this place until I bring the others back?" he asked, catching Carmichael's eye. The woman nodded and lifted her weapon.

"Long as the ammo lasts and they don't think to break out the cutting torches," she said simply. She looked at the bodies scattered about and the fallen weapons that littered the area and sighed. "First one is definitely not a problem, thanks to you."

"I aim to please. Now, I need the quickest way out of here that doesn't involve going through one of those doors. Any ideas?"

"There are maintenance passages running all along the curve of the hull. Mr. Pierpoint's idea…so workers could reach sections that had been sealed off by accident or electrical fault. You'll get dirty, but…"

"Better than getting dead," Bolan said. "Lead the way, Ms. Carmichael."

12

"This was...not part of the plan," Garrand said as his men fought to seal the door. He could hear gunfire echoing through the ship and knew that the cove wasn't the only breach in their defenses. The attackers were probably trying to climb the sides of the ship, as well. "We're being boarded by pirates. Actual, honest-to-God pirates. That is, well, unexpected. Where's Sergei?"

"Dead," Yacoub said. He coughed, rubbing at his watering eyes. He'd been caught on the edges of the explosion that had rocked the corridor and driven them back from the entrance to the cove. "Caught one in his thick skull."

"Good. One less thing to worry about." Garrand spoke into the radio clipped to his body armor. "All points, sound off." He needed to find out who was still in the game and who was already busy repelling the attack. A plan of defense was forming in his mind... find whoever was unengaged and use them as a flying squad to hit the closest attackers and smash them one by one. They were just fishermen, after all. No match for actual soldiers. Hell, half of them would probably get lost trying to find their way through the *Demeter*'s labyrinthine bowels. Voices crackled over the line with updates. He glanced toward the door as something occurred to him. "Where did they get stun grenades?"

"It's Somalia," Yacoub said.

"Yes, but those were M84 stun grenades. Not exactly standard issue," Garrand snapped. "Are we certain they're pirates?"

"What—fake pirates raiding fake pirates?" Yacoub looked at him as if he'd gone insane.

Garrand shook his head, wondering if he had. It was ridiculous, but, well, there was that nagging worry. He thought of the gunman who'd hit the control station. He hadn't been Somali, Garrand was sure. Could Pierpoint have hired someone, just in case? It was what Garrand would have done. A second team to wipe out the first once they'd served their purpose. No, he decided. Pierpoint didn't think like that. So… someone else then.

He shook his head, irritated by the mystery. "Never mind. We can beat pirates, Somali or otherwise. Fall back to designated strong points on this level. All points, hold what you've got, if possible. I worked too hard to take this bloody ship, and I'm not about to let it slip through my fingers without a fight." He signaled two of his men. "Right, Stanislaus, King, hold position here. Yacoub and the rest of you, come with me."

"Where are we going?" Yacoub asked as they hurried down the corridor.

"Hydroponics. We need to get to those prisoners before our guests do," Garrand said.

MACK BOLAN EASILY navigated the tight confines of the maintenance tunnel. He had traversed much more difficult terrain during the course of his War Everlasting. It was cramped but well-lit and ventilated. Every hundred yards, a circulation fan kept the air moving. Through the fans, he could see the interior of the ship and the armed men moving quickly in the opposite direction.

So far, he'd counted thirty. In situations such as this, it was best to assume the enemy had twice that number and act accordingly. Although Brognola hadn't been able to provide him with the schematics, Carmichael had pointed him in the general direction of the hydroponics bay, where the other prisoners were being kept. He'd marked his trail every few feet with a can of Day-Glo spray paint he'd looted from the boat quay. It was nominally used to mark the *Demeter*'s boats and Jet Skis, but it would serve well enough as road markers for the prisoners when he found them. With luck, they could follow his marks back to the cove, where Carmichael was waiting to take matters in hand.

When he found the access hatch he was looking for, he carefully opened it, mindful of noise. Luckily, the hatch must have been oiled recently because it opened without a sound, save the soft hiss of the seals disengaging. It swung outward, and Bolan eased himself onto the gantry on the other side.

He was struck by the warm, damp scent of green growing things as he moved along the darkened walkway. Blue and silver light illuminated what had once been a cargo bay, revealing orderly racks of green swaying in time to the subtle motions of the ship. The gantry was one of several that crisscrossed over the gardens, and a number of ladders reached up from the grated floor below.

Bolan paused and peered down, hunting for his quarry. He spotted them a moment later, his keen gaze picking out the bodies among the plant life. The hostages were corralled between two large, semicircular racks of plants, beneath the largest concentration of lights. Four men were watching them, all armed and alert. Every so often the radios they carried crackled as someone—probably Garrand—barked orders or demanded a sitrep. Bolan had considered taking a radio from one of the dead men in the cove, but they'd all been damaged.

This time he intended to do things a bit more carefully. Nonetheless, he would need to be quick. If he had been Garrand, the first thing he would have done was check on the other hostages to make sure they hadn't been freed or otherwise removed from play. Without the hostages, the mercenaries had no more leverage, and there would be no reason for the Maritime Patrol to maintain a distance. They'd move in, and it would all be over bar the shouting. Bolan had to free the rest of the captives before Garrand regrouped.

As the Executioner crouch-walked across the gantry toward the hijackers and their captives, he removed one of the trio of throwing knives from his combat harness.

The knives were light enough that Bolan could send them hurtling a great distance but heavy enough that they wouldn't bounce off their target. Crafted by Stony Man's own weaponsmith, John "Cowboy" Kissinger, the knives had been made according to Bolan's specifications. Although he preferred his KA-BAR combat knife, there were times the lighter knives were useful.

Raising the knife, Bolan took aim at the closest gunmen, a sallow-faced man who was smoking a cigarette. He let the blade fly with a snap of his wrist. It hissed home, only a few millimetres off target, tearing into the man's throat as he turned to yell at one of the hostages. He immediately clamped a hand to his throat, but to no avail. The dying man sank to one knee with a wretched gurgle, blood spurting between his fingers.

Even as he fell, Bolan popped the pin on one of his remaining M-18 smoke canisters. He sent it sailing over the heads of the remaining gunmen to bounce among the racks of greenery on the opposite side. It wouldn't distract them for more than a moment, but a moment was all he needed. As they turned, weapons opening up with a roar made cacophonous by the cavernous interior of the bay, Bolan caught hold of the gantry rail and vaulted over. He dropped the twenty feet with an ease born of training and bent his legs slightly to absorb the shock of the landing.

As the soles of his boots touched the deck, he opened fire with his Desert Eagle. The UMP was hanging by his side, out of the way. In a situation like this, where he had to contend with more than a few moving bodies, the pistol was more controllable. He fired twice, blowing one of the mercenaries backward into a rack, spilling plants and water across the deck. A woman screamed and men yelled as the hostages surged away from the violence like startled animals. The popping of the canister had set off the sprinkler system, and a light deluge peppered down, further decreasing visibility.

Bullets punched into the deck around him, and Bolan lunged between the nearest racks, moving low and quickly through the water and the smoke. He popped the pin on another M-18 canister and rolled it away from him. The remaining two mercenaries had split up and were moving cautiously through the racks, weapons raised. Bolan circled the closest, moving on the balls of his feet as he kept a rack between them. The mercenary was distracted by the smoke, the water and the screaming of the hostages, as Bolan had hoped he would be. Bolan heard the radio crackle and saw the man dip his head to answer. "Borjan here. We've got an intruder in hydroponics. I—"

Bolan saw no reason to let him finish. He whistled piercingly. The man—Borjan—whirled, eyes wide. Bolan fired the Desert Eagle, but Borjan was quicker than he'd anticipated. The gunman lunged forward, rather than retreating, and hit the rack with his shoulder. It groaned and wavered in its runnels, then balanced precariously for a long moment before it toppled onto Bolan, smashing him to the deck.

Bolan knew he was pinned the moment his back touched the deck, and he reacted accordingly, dropping his pistol and slamming his palms against the rack. With a heave of his shoulders and a twist of his hips, he sent the light metal structure tumbling away.

But as he freed himself, Borjan was on him, a combat knife in his hand. The mercenary was bleeding where Bolan's bullet had creased his cheek, but he didn't seem otherwise harmed. The blade of his knife bit into the deck as Bolan rolled aside. The Executioner rose to all fours and drove a kick into Borjan's shoulder, knocking him sprawling.

"He's over here!" the mercenary wailed as he scrambled to his feet. Bolan didn't waste time going for his Desert Eagle. Instead he swept up the dangling UMP and let off a quick burst, stitching his opponent from the hip to the crown of his skull.

Borjan toppled forward, the knife clattering from his hand. Before Bolan could locate his next target, a trio of hammer blows took him in the back and sent him facedown on the deck. His body armor had protected him, but even so, being shot hurt. He tried to suck air into his lungs.

Bolan heard the last mercenary approach and forced himself to remain still. His UMP was trapped beneath him. If he rolled over, his enemy wouldn't hesitate to shoot again, and this time, his body armor might not be enough to keep him alive. Bolan tilted his head slightly and caught sight of the hilt of Borjan's knife. Carefully, slowly, he slid his outstretched hand toward it, hoping that the water and the smoke would hide the movement from the approaching gunman. The footsteps grew louder. Bolan gritted his teeth and caught hold of the knife. Slowly, he pulled it closer. He heard the shooter stop. He could see the man's boots out of the corner of his eye. *Sloppy,* he thought. It wasn't a good idea to get that close to an enemy, even if you had shot them. Bad things could happen.

Like, say, someone putting a knife through your foot.

Bolan's hand whipped up and then down, as swift as a scorpion's strike. The knife slammed through the mercenary's boot with a crunch, and the man screamed. As he reeled, Bolan rolled onto his back, raised his gun and let off a burst. The mercenary fell, his foot still pinned to the deck. Bolan rose to his feet, rubbing his chest beneath his body armor. He was going to be sore for days. One more ache to add to his ever-growing collection.

"Still alive, though," he murmured. More than he could say for the men at his feet. Something rattled behind him, and he spun, UMP coming up. A hostage—one of the crew—stumbled back, hand raised. He was a lanky man with a nasty bruise on his cheek and a gun in his hands. Pleased that the man had taken the initiative, Bolan raised the muzzle of his weapon and extended a hand. "It's okay. Get the others. No time for explanations. We need to get everyone out of here."

"And go where?" the crewman demanded as he and Bolan hurried back to the others. There were eight of them. *Twelve in the cove,* Bolan thought as he pointed toward the gantry. That made twenty. But the soldier still didn't know exactly how many crew members were being held hostage along with the twenty passengers. And he couldn't forget Pierpoint.

"The maintenance hatches," Bolan said. "I've marked the path. Follow it, get to the cove." The man looked at him suspiciously. Bolan smiled grimly. "Tell

Carmichael I said hello." The crewman relaxed. Bolan
held out his hand. "Cooper."

"Jenkins," the crewman said, accepting the hand-
shake. "The others?"

"Everyone is still alive, as far as I know. I'm heading to the upper deck now. If you can get to the cove,
you should be all right. Take the guns and any ammunition you can find. The previous owners won't
need them." Bolan checked his own equipment and
made a quick calculation. He had two M-18 canisters
left and one M84. Three magazines for the UMP and
two for the Desert Eagle. And, of course, his remaining throwing knives and the combat knife. It would
have to be enough. Hopefully, Axmed and his men
had evened the odds somewhat. He looked at Jenkins.

"It won't take long for the bad guys to get here,
and I'd rather they not find us."

13

"Damn it, what's going on here?" Garrand shouted as he walked around the hydroponics bay. He could still smell cordite and the bitter odor of the spent smoke canisters. He looked down at Borjan and shook his head. He hadn't particularly liked the Serb, but he was fast running out of dependable guns. "How did they beat us here?"

"Not they," Yacoub said, crouching over one of the bodies. "Same ammunition, and I'd bet from the same gun. Somebody was shooting at us with a Heckler & Koch UMP-45 down in the cove, and that's what did it for Borjan and Antonio. Gordon got it with a Desert Eagle, unless I'm off the mark. And Tupper got a knife in the throat. What were you saying before about standard equipment?" He frowned. "Smoke canisters, stun grenades and now this…"

"We got a joker in the deck," Chuckles said. The American shook his head. "I know how he got in here, though." He pointed. "Maintenance hatches.

It's what I would do. Go all Nakatomi Towers on this here boat, you get me?"

Garrand nodded sourly. "This blasted tub has more hiding spots than I am entirely comfortable with." He sighed. "One of the pirates, then? We've got the rest of them contained, but one must still be loose, or else one of the prisoners…" He thought of Carmichael and the other crewmembers. Any one of them could be the culprit.

"Doubt that," Chuckles said. "They ain't got the stones. Maybe it's one of your money men, Garrand. Maybe they're trying to take advantage of the confusion. Or maybe Pierpoint hired somebody…an outside shooter. God knows who that guy has on speed dial."

Garrand opened his mouth and then abruptly closed it. Chuckles had a point. He wouldn't put it past any of their four "guests," especially Drenk or Gribov, to pull something like this. And he had his own suspicions about Pierpoint. He straightened. "Good point. Let's put a guard on them for the time being. Send more men to the cabana on deck. We've only got ten hostages left, and I don't want to lose them. And let's get this ship moving closer to the Somali coast, just in case."

"In case we have to run?" Yacoub asked.

"In case we have to sink the ship," Garrand said from between clenched teeth. "If I—we—can't have it, nobody can." He turned. "But first, we need to talk to Pierpoint. We need to find out who our mystery killer is and figure out a way to breach the cove's bulkheads without rupturing the hull." Either the prisoners or the pirates had sealed themselves in, and Garrand wasn't happy about it. The cove was the best way off the *Demeter* that didn't involve lifeboats and rappel lines. "Pierpoint knows the answer to both those questions... I'm sure of it."

Yacoub nodded and spoke into his radio, relaying Garrand's orders. Garrand blinked as something occurred to him. He looked at Borjan, then at the others. "Are any of them missing a radio?"

Chuckles did a quick sweep of the area and held up two fingers. "Borjan and Antonio's are borked, but Tupper's and Gordon's radios are gone." As he spoke, Yacoub stopped talking and stared at his radio. He cursed.

"They probably heard everything," he said.

Garrand raked his hands over his short-cropped hair. He wanted to curse, to scream his frustration at the solid walls of the bay, but he restrained himself. It wouldn't do to give in to such urges. His men were nervous enough.

The plan was in tatters, but he could still make it work. He had to make it work, or else all his efforts would have been for nothing. *Well, not nothing,* he thought a moment later as he recalled the satchel of ransom money Pierpoint had brought. It was safely stowed in the control room, out of sight and out of mind of everyone save Yacoub. Garrand glanced at his second-in-command, considering. It was a lot of money, even split two ways. One way would be better, but two was preferable to splitting it with anyone else.

No, not yet. I can still pull this off, he thought, dismissing the calculations he'd been making. They had the remaining hostages and Pierpoint. They had the *Demeter*, or most of it. And he had the promise of millions from his money men. All he had to do was sell this heap to the right sucker, and then it was someone else's problem.

"NOT MY PROBLEM," Pierpoint said, smiling thinly. "I told Yacoub you were biting off more than you could chew, and if you'd come to see me before now, I'd have said the same thing. You started this ball rolling, Georges. You can't blame me if it doesn't go where you'd like."

"It's been a busy few days," Garrand said. "You're lucky—you get to just sit here, staring at the wall." Pierpoint sat on his bed. Yacoub and Chuckles stood or sat around him, occupying most of the free space in the cabin.

Pierpoint glared at him. "Let me out, and maybe I'll give you a hand," he said with a glare.

Garrand laughed and waggled a finger. "Now, now, I said I was busy, not stupid." He looked around the cabin, examining the plethora of nautical-themed prints on the walls. "I need to know if you hired anyone else. Another mercenary from your oh-so-populated Rolodex."

"Why makes you think I know another mercenary?"

"You know more than one reporter. You know more than one movie star, more than one state senator, more than one member of the European Parliament. Why would you not know more than one mercenary?" Garrand countered.

"What makes you think I'm going to tell you?"

"If you don't, I'll hurt you," Chuckles said and flexed his hands.

Pierpoint shook his head. "Do your worst. I've been hurt before."

"Not like we can hurt you," Chuckles said softly.

Pierpoint shifted uncomfortably. "Maybe so." He swallowed. "But I doubt you have time." He glanced at Yacoub. "It's just like I said. You've lost control of the situation. Hell, you never even had control. I thought you were smart, Georges. I see now that your intelligence was overestimated."

Garrand blinked. He nodded, then lunged, his hands closing about Pierpoint's neck. For a moment, all his thoughts of the plan, of getting out of this with his original goals intact, were washed aside by a spurt of raw, red anger. It wasn't just Pierpoint's face he saw, turning red and then purple in his grip. It was all of his previous employers, every one of them. All of them had been obstacles, preventing him from getting everything he deserved in this world. And here, at last, he was on the cusp of the biggest score of his sorry existence, and the obstacles were still piling up.

Yacoub and Chuckles caught hold of him and dragged him back, prying his hands off Pierpoint's throat. "God damn it, Georges," Yacoub bellowed. "We need him alive!" Garrand tried to shove them off, but it was two to one, and they made too much sense. The fight went out of him like air out of a balloon.

"Alive," he muttered, glaring at Pierpoint, who lay gasping on his bed, one hand rubbing his bruised throat. He wasn't smiling anymore. "Yes, we need you alive, Pierpoint, but not in one piece… Don't forget that," he spat. He straightened and turned to Yacoub. "We're not going to get anything out of him. If he hired someone else, we'll deal with it. If it's some third party, well, we'll deal with it regardless."

"What about the cove?"

"Forget it. Shoot anything that comes out, but I'm not dividing the forces we have left to bang on a locked door. We've got pirates to roust. I want men on this door—and you, Yacoub. Watch him. If our killer *is* on his payroll, he'll be coming here soon. If he does, you take him." Garrand headed for the door, Chuckles in tow. "Let's see to our guests. I bet they're getting restless."

Yacoub said nothing as they left. Garrand hadn't missed Pierpoint's comment about speaking to his second-in-command. It was probably nothing. But Yacoub had always been susceptible to straight talk. He had an inherent distrust of complex strategy. *But he's never wavered...not yet,* Garrand thought. He hoped Yacoub wouldn't do so now. Not when they were so close.

"Well?" Pierpoint said. "What did I tell you?"

"Quiet," Yacoub snapped. He'd taken possession of a chair and was sitting, running his hands over his head. Pierpoint fell silent. The cracks he'd noticed earlier in Yacoub's calm had widened. When he'd first heard the gunfire, he'd hoped it had been a rescue attempt. Now he wasn't so sure, but whatever it was, he might be able to use it to his advantage.

He went to the desk and poured himself a glass of wine. As he sipped it, he wondered about the man Garrand had mentioned. Had someone in his organization hired another mercenary to rescue him? Or was it someone from the government, coming to scuttle the *Demeter* and hide all evidence of their support of his green initiatives?

The last was more likely, he suspected. At the thought of a CIA assassin clambering about the *Demeter*, looking to sink it and possibly Pierpoint himself, he almost wished Garrand luck in finding the man.

Whatever was going on, he still had his own goals to consider. The *Demeter*, and the work he'd put into it, couldn't be allowed to fall into the hands of drug dealers or terrorists. He'd sink it before he allowed that to happen. His mind turned to the engine room and the control panel that activated the voluntary scuttling mechanism. At the twist of a key and the pull of a lever, certain panels in the hull would open, allowing in the water.

It was another green improvement. A way of turning the shell of the *Demeter* into a breeding ground for reefs when its time was done. Once the hull panels were open, the ship would flood and the added weight would pull it down. The procedure was meant to be done closer to shore, and out of the shipping lanes, but Pierpoint saw precious few other options. Unless he could somehow make a deal with Yacoub or, failing that, one of Garrand's other men. If he could make contact with the crew…no. That wasn't likely. Pierpoint sucked on his lower lip for a moment, considering. Then he decided to take another shot at widening the crack between his captors.

"I didn't hire anyone, you know," he said after a moment. If he could get out of the cabin, he could lose himself in the belly of the ship. No one knew it better than him. No one would be able to catch him before he started the scuttling process.

"What?"

"This—whoever he is—you're looking for? Not one of mine." Pierpoint finished his wine. "No matter what Garrand thinks, I wouldn't sink my own boat. Not with all of these people still aboard."

"Who said anything about sinking the boat?" Yacoub demanded.

"Why else would someone sneak aboard this ship? I had…partners in the design phase. You know that, right?" he asked, pouring himself another glass. "They certainly wouldn't want their involvement to be made public. And if Garrand sells this ship…well." He shrugged. "Then, maybe I'm wrong. Maybe it's just an unusually determined pirate."

Yacoub frowned. "What sort of partners?"

"What, something Garrand doesn't know?" Pierpoint said. "Big partners. Powerful people, with lots of pull and far too many guns for my taste." He whistled a few bars of "The Star Spangled Banner" and smiled as Yacoub's eyes widened.

"Shit," the mercenary said simply.

"Hip deep and steadily rising," Pierpoint agreed. He gestured to the wine. "Would you care for a glass?" Yacoub shook his head. "No? Well, as I said, I don't know for sure, but I suspect."

"Why tell me? Why not tell Garrand?"

"You're the best of a bad lot," Pierpoint said. *And the only one around to listen to my bullshit.* "I've always respected you, Yacoub. I said that before and I meant it. If Garrand's 'mystery killer' is what I suspect, then the *Demeter* will soon be heading down into Poseidon's realm. One way or another. But that doesn't mean we have to go down with it." He gestured to the mercenary. "You and I, we could get out. I could vouch for you. I offered you Garrand's old job before. That offer still stands."

Yacoub made a face. "This again?"

"Why not? What has working with Garrand gotten you but trouble?"

"I should shoot you in the leg for that," Yacoub said. He patted the weapon holstered on his hip. "Then again, we are on a ship—mutineers walk the plank, don't they?"

"Or get keelhauled, neither of which you're going to do," Pierpoint said, rubbing his throat. "He's coming unglued, Yacoub. You saw it. You know as well as I do…"

"Shut up, Pierpoint."

"Last chance. I'm your only way out of this trap," Pierpoint said softly. He let the threat hang in the air for a moment. He knew the mercenary wouldn't hurt him; Garrand would've, or one of the others, but not Yacoub. He was too cautious.

"No, it's your last chance. Shut up, or I'll shut you up."

Too cautious, Pierpoint thought sadly. He tapped the wine bottle and looked at Yacoub speculatively. *Guess I'll have to do this on my own after all…*

"WHAT IS THE meaning of this?" Gribov demanded. "We are not children to be herded about." He lurched up from his chair, big hands curling like talons. Behind Garrand, Chuckles stiffened. "I am going nowhere. Unless you think you can make me…"

"I think I can shoot you," Chuckles said, patting the weapon slung across his chest.

Garrand waved him to silence. The last thing they needed was to set Gribov off. They were already fighting a war on two fronts.

"This is for your own safety, I assure you, gentlemen. The *Demeter* is currently under attack, and I would not see you harmed," he said. Drenk sat up, eyes narrowed.

"Attack? The Maritime Patrol?" he demanded.

"No, merely an overly enthusiastic band of local fishermen," Garrand said. "We'll have it taken care of in a few hours, perhaps less." As he spoke, a rattle of gunfire echoed through the stateroom, causing Kravitz to flinch.

"Savages," he murmured, patting the concealed shape of his shoulder holster.

"Fools, you mean," Walid said. "Just as we are fools to have come aboard this ship alone. You swore our safety was guaranteed, Garrand," he snarled. "The Black Mountain Caliphate will have your scalp if I am so much as bruised."

"Yes, well, the Black Mountain Caliphate will have to get in line, won't they?" Garrand replied, suddenly tired of playing the genial host. If not for the money, he'd have tossed all four men overboard. Some of them twice. "I am well aware of what is at stake, gentlemen. If you wish to waste your breath on threats, by all means do so, but it will not change my mind. You are going to a more defensible position, where I can keep an eye on you and where you will be well-defended from any potential danger."

"And we thank you for your efforts, Monsieur Garrand," Drenk said as he pushed himself to his feet. "Forgive my earlier tone. I was simply startled by the sudden change of situation. I have every confidence you will soon have this matter in hand and we can renew negotiations for the purchase of this fine vessel."

"You mean my purchase, don't you?" Gribov said.

Kravitz cleared his throat. "We have not, as yet, concluded the negotiations, Mr. Gribov." The Russian laughed and waved a hand.

"I think otherwise," he said. He looked at Garrand. "Are you certain we cannot…help in some way? For myself, it has been too long since I participated in a cleanup operation. I would gladly follow orders…"

I doubt that, Garrand thought. "No need, I assure you. Now, if you'll all follow me, I'll see you to the safe room." He turned to Chuckles and said, "Get up on deck. Keep it tight. We cannot lose those hostages, you understand?" he murmured. Chuckles nodded and left.

Garrand watched the four men gather their belongings, fighting to hide his impatience. If any one of them was going to try something, now would be the time. He was almost disappointed when none of them so much as stepped out of line as he led them down a level to the crew cabins. The purser's office was here—a full cabin with a lockable door and no porthole. Only one way in or out.

As he showed them inside, he said, "I'll send someone to get you as soon as things have quieted down." He closed the door before any of the four could reply. Garrand looked at the two men he'd brought with him. "Watch this door. No one exits or enters except Yacoub or me. Do you understand?" The men nodded, and Garrand smiled.

Now all he had to do was see to their mysterious commando. Whoever he was, and whoever he was working for, he was dead. Garrand intended to see to that personally.

14

Bolan navigated the maintenance tunnel swiftly, heading for the next deck up. Carmichael had told him there was a hatch in the floor where he could come out and surprise anyone unfriendly. The soldier could hear gunfire and yelling every so often, and more than once his new radio had crackled, delivering welcome information.

Bolan knew where most of the mercenaries were, and where they weren't, which was going to come in handy when he went back to retrieve the heavy duffel full of explosives he'd stashed two T-junctions back. He'd taped the bag to the side of tunnel, so it wouldn't be visible from the nearby vents. Hopefully, that would be enough to keep it safe until he could retrieve it. First, however, he had to get the last of the hostages to safety.

And Pierpoint, as well. *Can't forget the billionaire who'd caused all of this,* Bolan thought. People with too much money and too little sense were responsible for a good many of the world's ills. Most weren't criminals, but then, selfishness wasn't a crime. However, the things you did in the name of selfishness could make you a criminal. Garrand, for instance, had decided to hijack a ship and take innocent people hostage.

Metal creaked somewhere ahead of him. He froze, every sense straining, alert for any other sound. The tunnels weren't without their noises, but this one had been different. There had been a weight to it, not just the heat and the sea breeze making the metal flex. Slowly, he reached for his UMP. If someone was in the tunnel ahead of him, they were in for a nasty—

Bolan was rolling away, even before he'd completed his thought. The tunnel shook, and the metal sides and floor ruptured as a storm of bullets tore through it. Bolan pressed flat against the side of the tunnel closest to the hull. When the firing stopped, he scrambled back toward the last T-junction he'd passed through.

"Still alive, my friend?" someone shouted from somewhere ahead of him. The man spoke with a trace of a French accent, and he sounded like a carnival barker. *Garrand,* Bolan thought. He didn't reply. Instead, he continued to back away until he reached the junction and rolled out of the main tunnel.

"I bet that came as something of a shock, no? It was a good trick, I think. Not quite good enough, but *c'est la vie.* Once I figured out what you were up to, it was a simple matter to calculate your route," Garrand continued, his voice carrying through the tunnel. "And once I did that, well, you became the proverbial rat in a trap. There's nowhere to go, *Monsieur*...?"

Bolan said nothing. He peered behind him and then to the side. From the details Carmichael had sketched out, he knew that one tunnel of every such junction led to a hatch that opened onto the outside hull, all the way down past the waterline. He couldn't see any purpose for the hatches, but he said a silent thanks to whomever had decided to install them. Garrand might not have bothered to guard that one, reasoning that Bolan wouldn't be so quick to abandon ship. Decision made, Bolan started crawling toward the hatch. A rough plan was beginning to form in his mind. He was only a single level below the uppermost deck. If he could somehow climb up the outside of the hull, he could bypass Garrand entirely.

Of course, that still left the problem of how he was going to get the hostages out, but he'd cross that burning bridge when he got to it. He looked around and noted the hoses and power cables clipped to the top of the tunnel. Quickly, he drew his combat knife and sliced through a section of both, eliciting a shower of sparks and then a gush of fuel. Bracing himself, he stripped the cables and hoses free of their housings and began to twine them together, trying to ignore the spilling fuel.

"I can hear you scraping around, whatever your name is. No blood that I can see. You must be one lucky fellow. Not lucky enough, however. I've got men in the tunnels already. You're cut off. You can't go back, and you can't go forward."

"So I might as well give up, is that it?" Bolan called out as he worked. He needed to buy himself some time. If Garrand wanted to talk, they could talk. The longer they spoke, the less time they had to shoot at him.

"Ah! It speaks!" Garrand said. From the sound of his voice, Bolan judged that he was nearby, probably behind several of his men. Bolan considered tossing a stun grenade but then decided against it. He might need them later. "May I ask your name?" Garrand went on. "Or rank, perhaps? Serial number? Something?"

"Cervantes," Bolan said.

"Ah. *Don Quixote*, no?" Garrand laughed. "Apt. You are tilting at windmills, after all."

"I was thinking more of Lepanto…" Bolan grunted as he tied off a knot of wire. He jerked on it and then moved to the next.

"What?"

"Largest naval battle of the medieval world? Cervantes was there with the Spanish contingent," Bolan said. He looped the makeshift line over his shoulder and began to edge toward the hatch. "He didn't do much, mind, but he was there."

"Forgive me, but I'm not following you."

"We're on a boat," Bolan said.

There was a moment of silence and then Garrand laughed. "Clever, if a trifle obtuse," he said. "Wasn't Cervantes also imprisoned for several years?"

"Yes," Bolan replied. He could hear movement. He hadn't been the only one hoping to distract his opponent. He blinked tears out of his eyes. The fumes from the fuel line were filling the tunnel, and the smell was beginning to become impossible to ignore. It was time to move. He reached the hatch and pulled on the unlocking mechanism.

The hatch refused to budge. Bolan slammed his shoulder into it, again and again until his whole left side was numb. The seal bulged but refused to break. He looked around and caught sight of a panel set off to the side. He lunged for it and then jerked back as a bullet bounced off the tunnel curve. Shaking his hand, he turned and fired beneath his arm, back down the tunnel. The roar of the UMP nearly deafened him, but it achieved the desired result. He heard a yell and a clatter that could only be a fallen weapon. There was no way to tell whether he'd killed the man or not, but as long as he wasn't being shot at, he didn't care.

Bolan went for the panel again, flipped it open and saw that he'd been correct. He hauled down on the emergency release and heard the telltale hiss of pressure seals deflating. Behind him, someone shouted. He turned, pressing his back to the hatch to brace himself as he returned fire. With his free hand, he dug around in his gear for the book of waterproof matches he carried. Bolan needed a distraction while he made his escape, and the still dripping lubrication fuel would do as well as anything.

Bullets struck the frame of the hatch as it swung down, nearly spilling Bolan into the sea. Without hesitating, he caught hold of the frame and hauled himself out, leaving a lit match behind. A bullet clipped the heel of his boot, and for a moment, his entire foot went numb. He dangled in the air, trying to regain his balance. The match caught on the spilling fuel, and as he drew himself up, a gout of flame shot out of the hatchway. Bolan smiled. The fire wouldn't go far; the ship had emergency cutoffs for just such an occurrence, but it would hopefully put the fear of

God into Garrand and his men and keep them off his back for a few minutes more. Long enough for him to get to the deck.

Balanced on the outer frame of the hatch, he slowly stretched himself up along the hull and extended the improvised line of hose and wire as far as his arm could reach. It slipped through the rail on the third try, and with a jerk of his wrist, he caused the KA-BAR to turn sideways into an improvised anchor. He gave it a jerk, testing its tensile strength.

It wouldn't hold his weight for long. Gritting his teeth, the Executioner set his foot against the hull, and slowly, he began to climb, hand over hand.

"PUT THE FIRE OUT! Put the fire out!" Garrand howled, dropping out of the maintenance tunnel onto the gantry. Flames clung to his fatigues. The tunnel had been liberally doused with fuel. He'd noticed it but hadn't considered that Cervantes, whoever he was, would be crazy enough to set it alight.

Apparently, I was wrong. Again, he thought sourly as he rolled about on the gantry, slapping at the flames. Men stepped over him, expelling the contents of fire extinguishers up into the tunnel. Those men still inside were beating at the flames with their hands, or else scurrying for the closest access hatch. Garrand pulled himself to his feet. He'd underestimated his foe, and that irked him to no end. He prided himself on having a plan for every occasion, but this man, whoever he was, was making a mockery of that.

Even the best laid plans, he thought. He needed to think. He needed to try and predict where Cervantes would go next, now that he knew he was being hunted. He needed—

A shot struck the gantry rail, causing him to whirl. He drew his sidearm in the same motion and put two rounds in the raggedly dressed pirate who'd been rushing down the gantry toward him. More of them clustered at the nearby bulkhead, weapons trained on the surprised mercenaries. Garrand barked orders and fired again as the pirates opened up. One of his men screamed and fell from the gantry to the deck below.

The rest of his men reacted with commendable speed, forgetting about the fire above and raising their weapons. But they were in a bad position, completely exposed and too cramped to maximize their firepower. He tapped two of the closest men on the shoulder. "Fall back to bulkhead B-6. Go! Go!"

They squeezed past him and ran down the gantry. Once they'd reached the bulkhead, they could cover the others. Garrand tapped another man when he'd judged enough time had passed. "Bulkhead B-6, now," he said, pulling the mercenary past him. Only two left now, plus him. If they turned and ran, they'd all get bullets in the back. He tapped them both as he extended his pistol over their shoulders. "Suppressing fire. Ease back, and keep it to a trot. Keep their heads down."

He glanced up at the maintenance tunnel as he began to back away. The men in the tunnels would need to look after themselves. There was nothing more he could do for them.

15

Bolan ran along the edge of the pool toward the cabana, bullets biting at his heels. He'd come over the rail, right into the middle of a small war. Mercenaries on one side, pirates on the other. The latter had taken cover in the cabana, right where the hostages were supposed to be. Bolan, caught between both groups, decided to err on the side of his mission. So he ran, and the mercenaries obligingly gave him some encouragement.

He slid over one of the few tables still standing and caught the edge of the bar with his fingers. With a single, convulsive heave he swung his legs and body over the bar and crashed down behind it as a flurry of shots tore into the spot where he'd been perched.

About six pirates were huddled behind the bar, looking the worse for wear. Several of them had weapons aimed at him, and he was glad they'd decided to hold their fire. Axmed was among them, a bloody rag tied around one bicep. The pirate grinned as Bolan caught his eye.

"Ha! There you are! I was wondering where you had gotten to," Axmed said as he emptied the spent brass from his revolver into his palm. He caught Bolan's look and said, "Good casings are expensive. I try to be frugal."

Bolan shook his head and fired over the bar. A mercenary staggered and toppled into the pool. Axmed cheered. "When you meet the Devil, ask after my grandmother," the pirate yelled. He grinned at Bolan. "A very bad woman, my grandmother."

"Taught you everything you know, huh?" Bolan said.

"Ha! Yes, quite so." Axmed quickly reloaded his pistol. "You got here just in time. We were about to sweep them from the deck and into the sea."

Bolan glanced at the dead bodies scattered throughout the cabana. The pirates had taken a beating; their lack of discipline and body armor was beginning to show. Axmed's men were tough, but they weren't cut out for this sort of slugging match.

Axmed must have seen the look on his face because he sighed theatrically as he popped the cylinder of his weapon back in place. "Not as hard as I thought you were, Cooper. God must smile upon you for you to have survived this long." He shook his head. "All men die, and poor fishermen more often than most. If it makes you feel better, most of these men would have cut your throat for the equipment you carry the moment you let your guard down."

"Including you?"

"Especially me, my friend." Axmed slapped him on the back. Bolan winced as the blow came perilously close to the bruises that marked where he'd been shot.

Axmed rose to one knee and extended his arm over the bar to fire. Bolan joined him. The Executioner picked his shots carefully, trying to conserve ammunition. There were plenty of guns lying about, but he didn't like to rely on unfamiliar weapons. They had a tendency to jam at the wrong moment.

When the mercenaries returned fire, Bolan and Axmed fell back behind the bar. "I trust you have a plan," the pirate said. "I am getting tired of sitting back here. Too many splinters."

"Where are the hostages?" Bolan asked, checking the magazine of his UMP.

"Locked themselves in the freezer when they saw us coming," Axmed said with a shrug. "So much for gratitude, hey?" Bolan looked at him. Axmed laughed. "What? We might have been coming to rescue them."

Bolan shook his head and glanced at the freezer. It was a big walk-in job, like a deli might have. Enough room for ten people if they weren't disinclined to squeeze up. It was also probably the next best thing to bulletproof. Someone had made his job easier. The hostages were safe for the moment.

The fire from the mercenaries' side of the deck slackened abruptly and then fell silent. Bolan cocked his head and pressed a finger to his lips. Axmed nodded and flung out an arm, ordering his men to cease fire. Bolan could hear shots echoing up from elsewhere on the *Demeter*, but on the top deck, all was quiet. Then, someone called out, "Anybody speak English over there?"

Bolan gestured to Axmed. The pirate pressed his fingers to his chest, as if in surprise, and then inclined his head. He stood slowly, wary for a trick. "I believe I speak adequate English for the purposes of debate, yes," Axmed called out.

"What?"

"Yes, I speak English."

"Right," the voice said. A mercenary stood up from behind one of the overturned tables. He had the big, corn-fed look Bolan associated with the Midwest, but he moved confidently, like a seasoned soldier. He held his rifle slung across his chest as he stepped out into the open. Axmed moved slowly to meet him. "Truce?" the mercenary said.

"What do you think this is?" Axmed asked, flinging out a hand. "We have plenty of ammunition left, if you were wondering."

"I want to discuss surrender," the mercenary said.

"Excellent! Lay down your weapons and line up on deck."

"And they call me Chuckles," the mercenary said. He shook his head and poked a finger into Axmed's chest. "Your surrender, I mean. Your buddies below decks aren't going to last much longer. The cove is sealed off, and that means you ain't getting back to your boats. You could always go over the side, I guess, but either way…you're screwed."

At the mention of the cove, Axmed couldn't restrain a hard glance at the bar. Bolan knew the pirate was looking at him, and he fought to restrain a grim smile. But Axmed wasn't as quick as he thought he was. "Well, you appear to have all the cards. Why bother with surrender? Why not just kill us?" Axmed asked sourly.

"Why waste the resources?" the mercenary said.

He tapped the radio pinned to his vest. "Besides, I've got orders. If you're willing to stow your guns, we might consider…cutting you in. On all of this."

Bolan tensed. He hadn't expected that. And he had no idea which way Axmed would jump. From the look on his men's faces, the pirates didn't either. The closest of them eyed Bolan warily, obviously wondering if he would turn his weapons on them if Axmed agreed. Bolan didn't look at them, but he let his fingers drift toward his last stun grenade. It would have to be quick. He would probably take a bullet nonetheless. They were too close for him to escape entirely unscathed.

"Cutting us in, you say?" Axmed said after a moment of hesitation, hands on his hips. "Now that is interesting. That you have made this offer tells me many things."

"Yeah?"

"Oh yes. You see, a pirate learns quickly that the tastiest prey is often the most dangerous. You wouldn't be offering us a deal if you had the capacity to punish us for not accepting it. Why share this bounty…unless you have no choice?" Axmed said. He grinned. "I am guessing…low ammunition, low numbers and a distinct worry about the proximity of the Maritime Patrol?"

"You're smarter than you look," the mercenary growled.

"And you're stupider, if that's possible." Axmed laughed. His hand flashed to the back of his belt, where a heavy fisherman's knife was sheathed. He drew it and had it pressed to the mercenary's throat so quickly Bolan almost couldn't follow it. "And slow. Not a good combination."

The mercenary stiffened, his face frozen in an expression of surprise. "Well…shit," he said hoarsely. Axmed nodded cheerfully.

"Yes, quite so. Tell your men to drop their weapons, or I will open your throat, hey?"

"Gotta say they won't. We ain't exactly all for one, one for all, you dig?" Chuckles said.

Axmed shrugged. "Then we are at an impasse, no?"

"Yeah…no." The mercenary moved. He was fast, and smart, regardless of what Axmed had said. He tripped backward, his weapon coming up to fire a few wild shots. Axmed leapt into the pool as the other mercenaries opened up on the cabana again. Bolan could feel the bar shudder with every shot that struck it. Axmed was full of surprises.

He pulled his last M84 free of his combat harness and plucked out the pin. Then he rose to his feet and heaved the canister toward the mercenaries. It bounced once, twice and landed at the feet of the mercenary called Chuckles. He stooped, as if to scoop it up, and Bolan fired, spinning him around and into the pool. The grenade went off, filling the air with noise and light. Bolan moved around the bar, firing from the hip, picking his targets with care as he moved toward the pool. The water was red when he reached it, and a dark hand broke its surface. Bolan went to one knee and hauled Axmed out of the water. The pirate still had his knife in his hand.

"Chuckles indeed," he sputtered.

The pirates had followed him, as he'd hoped. Their

advance had sent the mercenaries into retreat. Axmed had figured right; they were likely low on ammo and short on time. A few more setbacks, and they might even abandon the boat. Axmed laughed.

"Between us, we might take this boat yet, eh, Cooper?"

"I'm not here to take anything," Bolan said, making to rise. He was stopped by Axmed's grip on his forearm.

"Maybe not. Is what he said about the cove true?"

Bolan considered lying. Then he nodded and said, "It is."

To his surprise, Axmed laughed. "And here I thought you were squeamish! Spence himself could not have foxed us better, my friend. Now we have no choice but to do as we swore or swim home, huh? Very well. Let it never be said that I am not adaptable." He clapped Bolan on the arm. "I presume we will be free to leave when you have secured the rest of the hostages, yes?"

Bolan nodded. "Once they're safely away, the ship is all yours, for as long as it stays afloat." He started back toward the cabana. "I'd secure the control room, if I were you. If you can figure out the controls, you might be able to get her into shallow waters. It'll make getting off easier when the time comes."

"Is that your professional opinion?" Axmed called after him.

"Just a hunch."

Quickly, Bolan went to the cabana freezer and knocked on the door as Axmed led his pirates away. Some of them peeled off to chase after the retreating mercenaries. Others followed Axmed toward

what Bolan thought was the command deck. Bolan
turned back to the freezer. No sound had answered
his knock. Carefully, he slid his knife into the locking mechanism and pried it open. He stepped back
as the door swung open.

The movement saved his skull as a full wine bottle
swept down through the space his head had occupied
only moments before. Bolan caught the bottle and,
with a twist of his wrist, he pulled it from its wielder's hand and threw it aside. "Relax, folks, I'm the
cavalry," he said. "I'm going to get you out of here."

"About damn time," the bottle swinger said as he
stepped out from behind the door, rubbing his hand.
He was a short, broadly built man of Hispanic descent. The Marine Corps insignia was tattooed on his
forearm, and he peered at Bolan in curiosity. "Who
sent you?"

"Does it matter?"

"Not really," the man said with a shrug. He stuck
out a hand. "Gonzalez."

"Cooper," Bolan said. "No time for small talk, I'm
afraid." He pointed to the lifeboats mounted on either side of the deck. "Those are your way out." At a
barked order from Gonzalez, the crewmen readied the
boats to be lowered. There were few of them among
this last group of hostages, but enough to keep the
situation under control.

Gonzalez, Bolan learned, had been the so-called
hospitality coordinator, and it was he who'd gotten everyone into the freezer when the shooting had started.
"Bulletproof," he said by way of explanation, knocking on the door as the others exited. "Damn thing

even has an air supply just in case you get locked in or the ship sinks. Pierpoint thinks of everything."

"Except pirates," Bolan said. Gonzalez laughed.

"Yeah, well, nobody ever expects pirates. Especially pirates you used to work with," he said. He hiked a thumb at the pool. "Chuckles bit it?"

"Was that actually his name?"

"I think it was Charles, but everybody called him Chuckles. No idea why," Gonzalez said with a frown. "It wasn't like he was funny or anything." He paused. "Maybe it was one of those 'fat guy called slim' situations…" He shook his head and looked out over the deck. "How long we got?"

"Long enough," Bolan said. "Garrand has his hands full right now, but once you get down, I need you to head for the prow and the cove."

"Yeah?" Gonzalez asked. He blinked. "The speedboats. Right, of course." He hesitated. "Did anyone…"

Bolan allowed himself a small smile. "With luck, they're waiting on you."

Gonzalez grinned in relief. "What about Pierpoint? I saw him arrive a few days ago, but nothing since then? He ain't dead, is he?"

"Not to my knowledge," Bolan said.

Gonzalez nodded. "Good. He ain't a bad guy, you know."

Bolan said nothing. He went behind the bar and found a coil of nylon line, most likely used to erect sun screens along the line of the immense mainsail. Slinging it over his shoulder, he headed back to the rail. He had no intention of shooting his way down to the next deck if he could help it. He knew roughly where Pierpoint was, and he intended to get there as quickly as possible, before Garrand had the same idea, at least. As he passed Gonzalez, the man said, "What about you? Aren't you coming with us?"

Bolan used the rail to tie off the nylon line, lashed the other end around himself and gave it a cursory jerk. "Not quite yet. Tell Carmichael that it's time to go. I'll get Pierpoint off if I can, but my job will be a lot easier if I don't have to worry about anyone else. And tell her to leave the doors to the cove open when you go. That's my route off this ship and if it's closed, I'll have to take my chances over the side. And I'm a bit rusty at my high dive."

Then, with a wave, the Executioner disappeared over the rail.

16

Bolan descended the side of the *Demeter*. Axmed's men had the mercenaries' full attention now, and both sides were trading shots on multiple decks. That left Bolan free to do what he needed to do. The safety line slid through his gloved fingers as he crept toward the porthole directly below him. As he descended, the lifeboats hit the water, carrying the last of the hostages to what he sincerely hoped was safety. They were out of his hands now. Luckily, most of Pierpoint's crew seemed competent enough.

Bolan peered through the porthole and saw two men standing in front of a door in the corridor beyond. Garrand wouldn't have bothered to put guards on an empty hallway. They looked distinctly nervous and far too alert for his taste. He needed to even the odds. The soldier unhooked his last smoke canister and pulled the pin before he pushed himself away from the hull of the ship.

The Executioner swung back and his foot con-

nected with the porthole, breaking the hardened glass
and popping it out of its seal. Swiftly, he tossed the
smoke canister through the hole and then, after a
whispered prayer, he eeled through himself, cursing
as his combat harness momentarily snagged on the
broken glass. Bullets pierced the smoke and chopped
into the wall over and around him. The protection
offered by the smoke wouldn't last long. He sprang
to his feet and surged forward, toward the last place
he'd seen the two guards. A bullet clipped the floor at
his foot, nearly sending him into a headlong sprawl,
but he continued on. Suddenly, a man appeared, eyes
wide.

Bolan slammed into him full-tilt. He smashed
the butt of his UMP into the mercenary's gut, dou-
bling him over. As the man bent, Bolan slammed the
weapon down on the back of his neck, flattening him.
A shot passed so close to his neck he felt the heat of
its passage and he whirled, drawing his knife.

His blade tore through black fatigues, drawing
blood and a high-pitched scream. A body lurched
back, wreathed in smoke, and Bolan followed with
all the surety of a leopard on the hunt. The second
mercenary crashed against the door of the cabin opposite, and Bolan drove his knife up through a gap
in the man's body armor and into his chest. Twitching hands clawed at his arm. The man stared at him
in uncomprehending horror as the light slowly faded
from his eyes. Bolan jerked the knife free with a single, smooth motion and stepped back. The body sank
and slumped forward.

Something clicked behind him. "Well, that was
uncomfortable to watch," someone rasped. Bolan

turned slowly and came face to face with the barrel of a Glock. A man frowned at him from behind the pistol. "I didn't know Stevens well, but I don't think he deserved that. I know of a few on this boat who might, but not Stevens." The man licked his lips. "You working for Pierpoint?"

"No," Bolan said.

"I didn't think so. One of the others, then. I told Garrand this was a bad idea, but did he listen? No, of course not. Nothing worse than a self-assured Frenchman. Don't move, or I'll blow your brains all over Stevens. He won't mind."

Bolan didn't move, but he was ready to do so at a moment's notice. He had his knife in hand, and his UMP, but the Glock was too close. The man's hand was trembling slightly but not from nervousness or strain. Bolan remained silent and waited for an opportunity to present itself. The mercenary sighed. "I ought to shoot you now, but Garrand will probably want to talk to you. Price I pay for friendship, I guess."

"Man should choose his friends with care," Bolan said.

"You're telling me," the mercenary replied.

"Yacoub," a third voice said. The mercenary half turned, and an empty bottle of wine nearly connected with his head. He jerked back just in the nick of time.

Bolan reached up and batted the pistol aside with the hand holding the UMP as he drove his knife toward the man's belly. Yacoub—if that was his name—caught Bolan's wrist, halting the knife inches from its target. His knee came up and connected with Bolan's thigh, causing him to stumble. Yacoub's head shot down to connect with Bolan's, and the soldier staggered, spots filling his vision.

Yacoub shoved him back into the door and swung his pistol toward the man who'd tried to clock him with the wine bottle. Bolan recognized Nicholas Pierpoint, pale with fear. The bottle fell to the floor. "Last mistake, Pierpoint," Yacoub growled. Before he could fire, Bolan shoved himself forward and slammed into the mercenary, swinging him across the corridor and into the door on the opposite side. They smashed through it in a cloud of splintered wood and hit the floor together, the pistol caught between them. Bolan had dropped both of his weapons and he clamped his hands on the pistol as they wrestled across the cabin floor.

Both men rose awkwardly, struggling for the weapon. Their momentum carried them forward, into the cabin's built-in closet. They smashed it to flinders. Yacoub forced him back, teeth bared in a silent snarl. The pistol went off, appallingly close to Bolan's face. The report nearly deafened him. He jerked the gun to the side, and it went off again, shattering the porthole.

Bolan freed one hand and drove stiffened fingers into Yacoub's solar plexus. The force of the blow was absorbed by the man's body armor, but even so, he took a step back. Bolan caught hold of his collar and pivoted, spinning the mercenary about and slinging him toward the en suite bathroom. Yacoub caught hold of Bolan's fatigues and they both fell into the door, bursting it off its hinges and spilling them into the cramped confines of the bathroom.

For a moment, they were caught in a tangle on the floor, both men barely able to move. Then Yacoub reached up and tore a cabinet door off its hinges and smashed it into Bolan's head. Bolan lurched back, and Yacoub's feet caught him in the chest. He crashed through the shower door and against the wall. Yacoub lunged for him. Bolan caught his hand and forced the barrel of the pistol against the wall. It roared again and again, filling the air with dust as it penetrated the shower wall. Bolan slammed Yacoub's hand against the broken edge of the shower stall until the pistol fell from his hand. Then he hauled the mercenary about and slammed him up against the shower unit, hard enough to crack the plastic casing. As Yacoub slumped, face bloody, Bolan caught hold of the hose of the shower head and looped it around his throat, as if it were a strangler's cord.

He hauled back on the plastic and metal hose as he drove a knee into Yacoub's back. The man gargled and clawed at the hose. Bolan pulled harder. His efforts were rewarded with the sound of collapsing cartilage and cracking bone as Yacoub's throat and vertebrae gave way. The mercenary bucked and kicked for a moment before he went limp. Breathing heavily, Bolan loosened his hold and let the body flop to the ground.

He looked up and met the eyes of the man he'd come to find. Nicholas Alva Pierpoint swallowed thickly and rubbed his throat as he looked down at the dead man. "Did you—did you have to kill him?"

Bolan didn't bother responding. Instead, he asked, "Are there any more? Or was it just three?"

Pierpoint blinked. "Ah…just—just the three, I think. Garrand doesn't have many men to spare.

Thanks to you, I'm guessing." He peered at Bolan. "I don't know you. Who are you working for?"

"That doesn't matter," Bolan said, pushing past Pierpoint to recover his fallen weapons. He paused in the corridor, listening. The sounds of gunfire had faded. That meant one of two things—either the fighting had moved away from this deck, or it was all over. Either way, it was time to finish what he'd started. Pierpoint followed him into the hallway, and Bolan grabbed his shoulder. "Come on. Time for you to abandon ship."

"What? No, I can't," Pierpoint said, twisting out of Bolan's grip. He held Yacoub's pistol in his hands, and he took aim at Bolan. "Not yet. The hostages, my people…"

"They're all safe," Bolan said. The pistol trembled in the billionaire's grip, as if he were uncertain of its weight. He held the weapon the way another man might hold a dangerous animal, as if afraid it would bite him. Bolan raised his hands, palms out. "Everyone worth a damn is off this boat or in the process of leaving. Except you and me. And once you're off, I can see about fixing this monumental screwup of yours," he continued.

Pierpoint gaped at him. "My screwup?"

"You're the one who concocted this scheme, aren't you? You're the one who decided to trust a psychopath like Garrand with the lives of your crew and your passengers, and all for what? Publicity?" Bolan asked acidly. "I'd say calling it a screwup is putting it politely."

"It was a good plan," Pierpoint said, backing away.

"I admit it had some…obvious flaws, but it was necessary for the good of the world!"

Bolan said nothing. Pierpoint swung the gun back and forth. One twitch and it would go off, whether the billionaire wanted it to or not. Bolan took a step forward, and Pierpoint's back struck the wall. "I've heard that before," Bolan said softly. "More than I care to think about. The fact is, you endangered innocent lives for no reason. If a good man hadn't asked me to save your sorry hide, I wouldn't have bothered coming after you. You and Garrand could have faced the sharks together."

"The sharks… You're going to sink the *Demeter*," Pierpoint said. He lowered the gun slightly. "You're going to scuttle her!"

"Damn straight," Bolan said. His hand shot forward, and he caught the barrel of the pistol. Quickly, he twisted it away from Pierpoint, who squawked in surprise. The Executioner pulled back the slide, ejecting the round in the chamber, and popped the magazine free. Then he tossed the weapon aside. "And if you give me any trouble, I'll send you to the bottom with her." He didn't mean it, but he wanted to impress upon the man the seriousness of the situation.

Pierpoint smiled widely. "Why didn't you bloody well say so in the first place?" he asked, beaming like a child on Christmas morning.

17

Mr. Drenk was many things, but a fool wasn't one of them. In his years of service to various Pan-Pacific criminal enterprises, Drenk had come to understand that all situations had a point where they became untenable. A moment—often swift and passing unremarked—where the odds shifted and survival became the objective rather than business. His ability to sense and capitalize on such pivotal moments had made Drenk the man he was. A man who knew when it was time to kick over the game board and make a different sort of play entirely.

As he sat in his chair, Drenk felt things shift, and he sighed. He cracked his knuckles, feeling the power in his fingers and wrists. He caught Gribov's glance and smiled thinly. Like him, Gribov was a pugilist. He liked to work with his hands. Tools felt alien. All a man needed was strong fingers and a stronger stomach, and he could do terrible things indeed.

Things Drenk would like to do to Garrand. The

mercenary was a shallow, sneering pantomime villain, all talk and promises but with no real power. He had stumbled onto opportunity but had no idea how to make the most of it. Drenk looked around and sighed again. *What I could do with this place,* he thought, and not for the first time since coming aboard. His masters might still let him have his way, but he doubted it. They too could only see the obvious—a more cost-efficient ship to smuggle with. Drenk, however, had ambitions beyond the smuggling of heroin and peasants.

What I could do, he thought again. A floating fortress, suitable for a warlord of the modern era. Staffed with a loyal crew, the *Demeter* could become a mobile staging area for any number of operations, drug-related or otherwise.

Garrand had had it all, and now he was letting it slip through his fingers. He had lost control of the situation the moment Drenk and the others had set foot on the deck. In fact, he'd never had control. Always boasting of his plan. Drenk shook his head. Plans were for fools and dreamers. Drenk never planned. He acted and reacted. That was enough.

"What is going on out there?" Walid demanded as Drenk stood and stretched. "What is it? Are we under attack?" They'd heard an explosion coming from the deck and before that, fire alarms squealing below. Now, they heard more gunfire, squawking radios and the quiet, worried conversation of the men guarding the door. The *Demeter* was a noisy ship, Drenk reflected.

"Who would be so foolish as to attack while there are still hostages?" Kravitz asked, frowning.

"Pirates," Gribov said lazily. "We are in the Gulf of Aden. These waters have a surplus of sharks and pirates. And this ship is a tempting target."

"Else why would any of us be here?" Drenk said as he looked around the cabin.

"We are here for a business transaction, nothing more," Kravitz said. He licked his lips nervously. The thin man stank of fear, and Drenk wondered when he would pull the pistol he had holstered beneath his arm. Both he and Walid carried guns, unlike Drenk or Gribov. Indeed, now would be the perfect time to clear the deck of opposing bids, were the situation a calmer one. But Drenk knew, without knowing how or even questioning that certainty, that there would be no more bidding. The *Demeter* was a floating battlefield, and it would go to the victor. Sitting in one place, waiting for the guns to fall silent, was a good way of assuring they would miss out on the prize entirely.

As he had so many times before, Drenk decided to seize the moment. His employers in the Black Serpent Society would reward him for securing this ship, and even more so if he did it without spending a penny. Drenk smiled and stretched his arms. His smile grew as he felt the blade hidden up his sleeve slide into his waiting palm. Now the only question was, who to sink it into?

Three choices. Only one chance. Who to pick, who to pick?

Drenk was good at sizing men up. He could walk into a room and pick out the most dangerous man in a heartbeat. Usually, it was him. In this case, it was a toss-up. Gribov was a monster, a skull cracker in the old fashion, a man who knew his way around truncheons and alligator clips. But the other two were dangerous, as well. Walid was erratic and a believer, always a dangerous combination. Kravitz was too controlled; when he popped, he might kill anyone.

Gribov caught his glance and showed his steel-capped teeth. There was an ugly light in his eyes that Drenk had seen before in the mirror. That light made his choice for him. Walid was panicking, Kravitz was worried but Gribov… Gribov had seen the moment, too. Gribov, like Drenk, knew what was happening, knew that opportunity had reared its scaly head and intended to do something about it.

"Out of my way," Walid snarled as he pushed past Drenk and started for the door. "I will not die here, like a street cur."

"No. You will not," Drenk murmured as he drove his knife up into Walid's back with a speed just this side of inhuman. The terrorist gasped and clawed uselessly at the air as Drenk slung him to the ground, yanking the knife free in the process. Kravitz gaped in shock, but before he could get to the pistol holstered beneath his arm, Gribov's big hands closed around his throat.

"No, my friend," Gribov rumbled as he slowly wrung the other man's neck. "No, today is not for little weasels, eh? Today is for wolves." He let the body fall and looked at Drenk. Gribov smiled. "To the winner, the spoils, eh?"

"Indeed." Drenk wiped his knife clean on Walid's trousers. "We should go see that our investment is not prematurely sunk, I think, by overzealous pirates or foolish mercenaries." He gestured with the blade. "After you…"

"No, no, after you," Gribov said amiably.

Drenk scooped up Walid's pistol from its holster, took aim and fired through the cabin door in a tight pattern. Gribov joined him, Kravitz's weapon looking tiny in his big hand. They fired until their respective weapons clicked empty. Then Gribov kicked the door off its hinges and stepped through.

They'd caught one of their guards by surprise, killing him instantly. The other had been quicker on his feet or simply more paranoid. He swung his weapon toward Gribov as he barked into his radio, but the big Russian was faster than he looked. He snapped forward, catching the weapon's barrel and smashing it aside even as it spat fire. His other hand drove forward like a piston, snapping the unfortunate mercenary's head back with a sound like a cracking branch.

"Only two," Gribov said. "Should we be insulted?"

"I look on it as good fortune rather than an insult," Drenk said. He scooped up the mercenary's weapon and checked it over. "As is this…full clip. How fortuitous."

"Guns are for the weak," Gribov said, tossing Kravitz's pistol aside.

"There are a lot of weak men on this ship, I think," Drenk said. "Let us go find their boss and see what he has to say about that."

"THIS…THIS IS a complete and utter disaster," Garrand said, looking down at Yacoub's body. Pierpoint's cabin was a wreck, and there were three bodies in the debris. Three more good men dead because he hadn't

planned for every contingency. Because he hadn't
planned for the man calling himself Cervantes. He
frowned and scrubbed at the burns on his clothing.
The fire Cervantes, or whatever his name was, had
set was still burning. It had spread to the hydroponics
deck, thanks to a few careless crewmen, and sprin-
klers were going off on three other decks. Smoke
was billowing out of portholes, alarms were screaming, and he couldn't raise any of the usual suspects.
What bothered him the most was how *quickly* it had
all fallen apart.

Thankfully, they had found the man's stash before
he had a chance to use it…and before the fire. Garrand looked at the satchel where he'd set it down. He
shuddered to think of what would have happened if
they hadn't. Then, maybe that had been Cervantes's
plan from the beginning. An explosion like that might
have ripped the guts right out of the ship.

Regardless, Garrand had it now, though God alone
knew what he was going to do with it. *I could use it,*
he thought. Cut my losses, send the whole mess to the
bottom of the sea, money, men and all. And wouldn't
that just be the cherry on top? He smiled sadly. "This
wasn't part of the plan, Yacoub. You have to believe
me." He sank into a crouch, hands dangling between
his knees, eyes on the slack features of his closest
friend. *We were friends, weren't we?* Or as close as
men like them ever came. Brothers in arms, maybe…

"I want you to know that I'm sorry," he said after a
moment. He'd come up here to take custody of Pierpoint himself. Pierpoint was his last bargaining chip.
The *Demeter* was as good as lost. There was no

telling how many pirates were running around. The galley, the guest cabins…lost and being looted as he stared at Yacoub's slowly cooling corpse. There was still the ransom money in the control room, of course, and the money men in the purser's cabin. Then the radio suddenly crackled. He heard shots and Gribov's voice, and he knew the latter was no longer the case. He pulled the radio from his vest and tossed it down. It was a gesture of surrender more than anything else.

"Well, that's torn it, I suppose," he murmured. He rose to his feet. "You were right, as usual," he said, looking at Yacoub. The radio continued to crackle as men cried for backup or told Garrand to go to hell, in no particular order. There weren't many men left, and they were pinned down, scattered across the *Demeter*. Yacoub had been right. Garrand had bitten off more than he could chew. There was nothing left to do but—

The radio spat. A familiar name rose out of the static. Pierpoint had been sighted. But why was he heading to the engine room? Garrand almost picked up the radio to reply, to ask for more info, but he didn't. Instead, he grabbed the satchel and stepped over Yacoub's body and out into the corridor.

The plan had failed, but he already had a new one. A simpler one, and he required only two warm bodies to pull it off. That had been his mistake from the first. *Keep it simple, stupid,* he thought, as he marched toward the elevators at the end of the corridor. They still worked but not for much longer, he suspected.

Whatever Pierpoint was planning, Garrand intended to see him dead first. Let the billionaire sink with his multimillion-dollar boat. If he couldn't have the money, satisfaction would have to do. *Sounds like a plan.*

As the elevator doors closed, Garrand smiled.

18

"Bombs would make a hash of it anyway," Pierpoint said as he and Bolan moved down the gantry staircase toward the *Demeter*'s engine room. Alarms blared throughout the ship now, and it lurched almost imperceptibly around them, groaning and creaking as its engines roared and bit at the water.

Bolan hoped the movement and the noise meant that Axmed had gotten to the control room. The closer they were to shore, the better the chance of survival for all of them, if what Pierpoint had told him was true. He still wasn't certain if he believed in Pierpoint's little scheme, but he was willing to give it a chance because he had no way of getting back to the explosives.

"I built her to survive multiple explosions," Pierpoint continued. "You'd have gutted her, sure, but she wouldn't have sunk. Not unless you got really lucky…"

Bolan, reacting with battle-honed instinct, caught

Pierpoint by his collar and hauled him out of the way as bullets struck the gantry then ricocheted off into oblivion. Bolan returned fire smoothly and was rewarded by a strangled cry. A mercenary slumped and fell to the deck. Bolan crouch-walked over to the body, checked for a pulse and then waved Pierpoint forward. There might be more mercenaries around, but they needed to keep moving.

"Then again, luck seems to be the one thing you don't have to worry about," Pierpoint murmured as he stepped over the dead man. He looked around, face pale. "Where are the rest of them? Garrand isn't stupid. He'd have more men guarding the engine room…"

"Fighting for the ship, I imagine," Bolan said. "Or, if they're smart, trying to figure a way off this boat." He looked at Pierpoint. "You're sure this will work?"

"Better than the explosives you claim to have stashed," Pierpoint said. "I built this boat with the knowledge that I was going to have to sink it one day."

"Seems like a waste of effort to me," Bolan said. But he suspected Gonzalez had been right about the billionaire. As arrogant, condescending and egotistical as he was, Pierpoint's heart seemed to be in the right place. Pierpoint snorted.

"You know what's a waste of effort? Oil pipelines. Fracking. This—the *Demeter*—this was a goddamn Hail Mary pass, and it almost worked, too. People are the key, Cooper. Get the people talking, get them interested, rile up the constituent base and suddenly, all those pie in the sky, unfeasible green initiatives get passed. Let a few reality show stars and gossip rag reporters cruise around the world for a few months, and all eyes turn to your cutting-edge hydroponics facility or your solar-powered engines, and Ma and Pa Kettle are wondering why oh why they don't have one of those." Pierpoint's eyes gleamed as he spoke. "It would have worked. *It would have.* But Garrand had to go and screw everything up. Stupid, short-sighted son of a—"

Bolan clapped his hand to Pierpoint's mouth and forced the other man back against the wall. Someone had silenced the alarms.

The emergency lighting still cast a dull crimson glow over everything, putting Bolan in mind of a nuclear submarine he'd once had the misfortune of boarding. He motioned for Pierpoint to remain where he was and slunk off into the thicket of pipes, consoles and pumps that filled the ill-lit confines of the engine room.

Bolan peered into the dark, searching out any sign of his enemies. If they were there, they had heard the shots that had taken down their compatriot. They would be waiting for him. He peered up, searching the gantry. If it were him, he'd have sought out high ground. He was rewarded by the telltale flash of metal and knew that his suspicions had been correct.

Moving slowly, he raised his UMP and swung under the gantry, eyes locked onto the steel mesh. He saw a body crouched above him, and he fired. The mercenary stood up straight as the bullets tore through him, then he tumbled from the gantry. Almost immediately, a bullet smacked into the pipe near Bolan's head, releasing a burst of steam that nearly blinded him as he sought cover. The radio he'd confiscated crackled as someone he assumed to be the shooter, given the background noise, requested backup.

Another shot clipped the deck near him and then bounced off into the dark. Bolan set his UMP between two pipes and pulled a coil of wire from his combat gear. He needed to smoke the shooter out, the sooner the better. He had no time to crouch in the dark trading shots. Carefully, he wrapped the wire around the trigger and let it unspool as he moved to the other side of the wide duct he'd taken cover behind. Sinking onto his haunches, he drew his Desert Eagle and gave the wire a quick tug.

The UMP snarled, piercing the red light with a flash of yellow. The unseen shooter fired in reply, chewing up the gantry and the pipework around the UMP and inadvertently revealing himself to his prey. Bolan rose, both hands on his Desert Eagle. He took aim and fired. The sound of a body thudding to the deck echoed through the jungle of metal and plastic. Bolan waited, counting the seconds until he was sure that was the end of it, and then he went to retrieve Pierpoint.

Pierpoint looked queasy as Bolan moved him past the bodies. "What a waste," he muttered. "I hired half of these guys. They never seemed…"

"They were mercenaries," Bolan said. "They knew the risks when they signed up with Garrand and decided to take part in this." *And most of them probably deserved worse than a quick bullet,* he thought. He'd met more than a few soldiers of fortune in the course of his war; some he'd worked alongside, and others he'd stared at through the scope of a rifle. Like anyone else, they were no better or worse than their actions. Garrand's men were probably worse than most. If they hadn't already been criminally inclined, they wouldn't have been on the boat in the first place.

"Maybe," Pierpoint murmured. He shook his head and started toward a smallish door set off from the main drag of the engine room. "Doesn't matter anymore, I suppose." He paused before the door. Bolan saw that a keypad lock had been set into the space above the handle. Pierpoint stabbed in a code and gave the handle a twist. The door swung inward with a hiss. "Or it won't in a few minutes."

He and Bolan stepped through into a smallish room. "Smugglers used to install mechanisms like these in their ships once upon a time. Wooden slats could be removed to flood a hold and sink a ship if the authorities started sniffing around, and then pumps could drain the water and leather bags full of air would raise the ship." Pierpoint paused, looking around at the assortment of pumps and levers. "Granted, their ships were a good deal smaller, but my engineers assured me that the principle was the same."

"Fascinating," Bolan said, keeping watch at the door. "Hurry it up."

"Keep your shorts on," Pierpoint said as he began to throw levers and twist keys. "I don't suppose the *Demeter* will ever resurface, though. Not if your bosses have their way." He shook his head. "It's funny, isn't it? The technologies on this ship could improve the lot of the common man, but it has to stay sunk."

Bolan didn't reply. He wasn't in the mood for a lecture. Politicians were outside his remit, unless they'd killed someone or were otherwise a danger to innocent life. He looked up as a hollow clanging suddenly

echoed through the ship. Pierpoint laughed. "There
we go, like the bells of doom." He looked at Bolan.
"The hatches are opening. We should go."

"How do you know it worked?"

Pierpoint gestured. Bolan turned and saw water
spilling across the deck from somewhere out of sight.
His nose stung from the sudden scent of salt water. The
lights began to flicker and a new alarm, different to
the other, began to sound. "The bottom hatches open
first," Pierpoint said. "Like I said, time to go."

They hurried toward the stairs, Bolan keeping
Pierpoint on his feet as the ship began to shudder and
moan about them. The water rose as they climbed the
stairs, white froth swirling at their heels. They hurried through the doorway that led to the cove, and the
water was there to greet them as the hatches on that
level opened. "Pick up the pace," Bolan growled. "I'd
rather not drown, if it's all the same to you."

"I hope Carmichael and the others made it off,"
Pierpoint said as Bolan propelled him along. "Should
we have given them more time?"

"Any more, and we risked losing our chance to
sink this tub," Bolan said, though privately he was
wondering the same thing. He hoped Carmichael and
the others were as competent as he'd thought. "One
way or another, we'll find out in a minute."

They were in the home stretch now, the water
clutching at their shins. The cove was two doors
away, and they would be there in minutes. He spared
a thought for Axmed as he shoved Pierpoint ahead
of him, and he wondered whether the pirate would
heed his warnings.

Pierpoint froze, and Bolan nearly ran into him. He

opened his mouth to say something and then closed it as he caught sight of the lean figure standing between them and the next door, a pistol in his hand.

The man smiled thinly. "Well, at least something went according to plan."

19

"Yacoub was my friend," Garrand said as he splashed toward them, pistol extended. In his other hand, he carried a heavy satchel that Bolan recognized easily enough. He restrained a curse. He'd been careless. Or else Garrand was smarter and luckier than he'd expected. "The only one, now that I think about it. One of the perils of my particular line of work, you see. Can't trust any of the other bastards in it. And you had to go and kill him." He glanced at Bolan. "I don't know you."

"You will," Bolan said.

"Cervantes." Garrand held up the satchel. "Thought that was you. Found your toys." He smiled but only for a moment. "Drop the UMP."

"You drop yours."

"Drop it, or I shoot Pierpoint." Garrand let the barrel twitch aside, so it was aimed at Pierpoint's chest. "He's who you came to get, isn't he? All this, just for that fool." He shook his head and sighed mockingly.

"I would have given him back eventually. I wouldn't keep him if you paid me. Which you have. Not as much as I'd hoped, but *c'est la vie*. He who dares, wins. And once I handle this last detail, I shall collect my earnings and depart for more salubrious shores."

"Money," Pierpoint said in disgust. "That's all you care about."

"Says the billionaire," Garrand retorted. "Yes, it's all I care about. What—I should care about you? The environment? No, money buys happiness, regardless of what the proverb says. My kind of happiness, anyway. And since you've killed everyone I might have split it with, I have quite a bit of happiness to buy once I go collect it. Thank you, by the way," he said.

"Happy to help," Bolan replied.

Garrand frowned. The corridor shook slightly, and the water was steadily climbing. He held up the satchel. "I was going to use your toys to gut this tub, but I see you beat me to it. I should have known. Always a bad one for sharing, weren't you, Nick?"

Pierpoint cursed and took a step forward. Garrand raised his weapon and clucked his tongue. "No, stay there. I think I'm going to seal you two in here instead. Save the bullets. You move, I shoot. You shoot me, well…" he held up the satchel "…that might get messy. Who knows what sort of toys you've got in here, hey, Cervantes?"

Bolan tensed. It wasn't likely that a stray shot would do anything more than perforate the satchel, but if Garrand had armed the explosives, then it was a different ballgame entirely. He considered his options. He might be able to get a shot off, but Pierpoint was in the line of fire. As the water lapped at his knee he frowned. He glanced around, trying to see something, anything that might help.

"That's right, just stay there," Garrand said as he backed away. "I hear drowning is just like going to sleep. Better than you two deserve, but, well, whatever gets the job done."

"My thoughts exactly," said a deep, mellifluous voice. Garrand spun and then staggered as a blow caught him across the chin. He stumbled back and tried to swing his gun around, but his attacker was on him in an instant. Garrand howled as his gunhand was pinned to the wall by an iron grip and a fist caught him in the side. Bolan grabbed Pierpoint and shoved him aside as the gun went off, roaring in the confined space of the corridor. Bolan heard Pierpoint grunt as he let go of the man's arm, and his guts turned to ice as he raised his weapon.

The Executioner hesitated and turned back toward the billionaire. He'd been too late. Pierpoint sagged into the rising water, his eyes going glassy as he gripped at his chest. Blood streamed from between his fingers and he tried to speak as Bolan caught him and leaned him against the wall. No words came out, only a harsh rattle. Whatever Nicholas Alva Pierpoint had wanted to say was lost in the rumble of the ship and the rising water.

Bolan heard Garrand laugh and then someone said, "Quiet, fool." There was a splash, and Garrand fell, face purpling from a blow. The man standing over him spread his hands and smiled at Bolan. "Ah, I am sorry." Bolan recognized Drenk from his mug shot and felt a cold calm envelop him. "Was he important?" He cocked his head. "Are you?"

"Kill him, Drenk! Kill him, and this boat is yours," Garrand sputtered, trying to pull himself to his feet. "Free of charge—just pull out his trachea for me."

"This ship is sinking, Monsieur Garrand, and of no use to me," Drenk said, never taking his eyes off Bolan. "But I intend to make you pay for my wasted time and for your casual disregard for the niceties of business. The Black Serpent Society does not suffer such insults gladly." Drenk flexed his fingers. "Who are you?" he asked Bolan.

Bolan rose to his feet, his UMP pointed at Drenk. "Nobody you want to know," he said slowly. He glanced down at Pierpoint and then at Garrand, who shrank back from the look in the Executioner's eyes. Drenk caught the look and laughed softly.

"The Chinese have a saying…dangerous men will meet in narrow streets." He fell into a stance Bolan dimly recognized, hands raised, knees bent. "I think you are a dangerous man. And I am not one to leave dangerous men unchallenged."

Before Bolan could reply, Drenk came in fast. He caught hold of a low hanging pipe and swung himself up. His feet snapped out and kicked the UMP from Bolan's grip with startling accuracy. Bolan back-pedaled quickly, the water lapping at his legs, and snatched for his pistol. Drenk dropped to the floor in a crouch and sprang toward the Executioner, his face a mask of anticipation. He caught Bolan's wrist and prevented him from pulling his weapon as he drove his forearm into the Executioner's windpipe.

Coughing, Bolan kicked Drenk's knee, knocking the man back. The two men split apart, breathing heavily. Drenk's fingers were stiff, like blades, as he raised his hands. "You're good," he said. "Not as good as me, but…passable."

"I'll take that as a compliment," Bolan said, sizing the other man up. Drenk was loose limbed and larger than he first appeared. Big hands, big feet, big head, knuckles like iron. Drenk slid forward, moving smoothly. His blow snapped out before Bolan even realized it was coming, and it danced across his belly. Bolan's body armor absorbed the brunt of it, but even so, his lungs strained for a moment. He swatted aside the next blow, redirecting its stinging force with his palms. Drenk closed in, every limb moving with lethal intent; he attacked in a whirlwind of knees, elbows, fists and feet.

Bolan knew his opponent was trying to keep him from getting to his pistol. But if he could put some distance between them, he might have a chance to end this quickly. Drenk, however, wasn't willing to give him any breathing room. The killer followed him as he backed away, battering at him. It was all Bolan could do to absorb the punishment and wait for an opening. All he needed was one instant of inattention and he could get the initiative back.

When it came, Bolan almost missed it. Drenk slid on something beneath the water, losing his balance. He regained it in a moment, but Bolan was already moving. He launched himself backward and groped for his pistol. But even as he drew it, Drenk was coming for him, teeth bared in a rictus of fury. Bolan fired, and the bullet tore open Drenk's cheek, just before the man crashed into him and they both went down into the steadily rising water.

Drenk's fingers sought Bolan's throat. Bolan's head connected with the floor, and his vision spiraled. Drenk's mangled face leered down at him. Black dots crowded at the edges of Bolan's vision, and he fought to avoid sucking in a lungful of water. Drenk leaned on him, using the weight of his body to pin Bolan beneath the water.

The Executioner twisted, bringing his knees up. He shoved them between his chest and Drenk's. Before his enemy could react, Bolan caught the back of Drenk's head and dragged him down as he lifted his knees. Kneecap connected with jaw, and Drenk's head snapped back. Bolan lunged up out of the water, his breath burning in his lungs. He drew his KA-BAR as he moved, and with a single, savage motion, he drove it into Drenk's belly as they went under the water. The killer folded over, grabbing Bolan's forearm in a painful grip. He glared at Bolan for a moment and then his features relaxed and his grip slackened.

Breathing heavily, Bolan hauled himself up. Water stung his eyes and rolled down his face, but he could breathe again. The same couldn't be said for Drenk. The killer had slid beneath the water, and only a cloud of red remained to mark the position of his body. Bolan rubbed his throat and stood.

"Well done," a heavily accented voice said. "And you've saved me the trouble of dealing with him. How excellent."

Bolan turned slowly, willing strength back into his limbs. Drenk had tested him to his limits, but the fight wasn't over yet. He grinned mirthlessly when he saw who his audience was. "Hello, Gribov."

The Executioner raised his fists. Gribov was between him and his weapon, and his combat knife was still buried in Drenk's belly, somewhere under the water flooding the corridor.

"I do not know you," Gribov growled, "but I think I hate you." He raised his hands.

"The feeling is mutual," Bolan countered.

"I will crush the life out of you with my bare hands." Gribov surged forward, fists a blur. Bolan absorbed the strikes on his raised forearms. Gribov punched like a mule kicked, and his blows came fast and steady despite the blood that ran down his craggy features. Water lapped at their shins as they danced back and forth, trading punches.

Gribov's fist barked against Bolan's chin, snapping the Executioner's head back. Bolan stumbled and slammed against the bulkhead. He caught Gribov's next blow and twisted the Russian's wrist sharply while squeezing his hand. Finger bones popped and cracked and Gribov spewed curses as he drove a solid kick into Bolan's belly. Bolan held on to his opponent's hand and continued to squeeze and twist, stretching ligaments and grinding bones together in his viselike grip. Gribov kicked him again and smashed an elbow down on Bolan's collarbone, nearly driving the Executioner to his knees.

Bolan yanked Gribov's hand to the side and bent his wrist back until it made a sound like ice cracking. Gribov yowled and clawed for Bolan's scalp. Bolan bulled into the other man and drove his head into Gribov's face. The killer's nose burst in a spray of red, and it was his turn to stagger. Bolan pivoted, dragging Gribov's arm over his shoulder at a sharp angle. The elbow joint popped like a gunshot, and Gribov grabbed for Bolan's throat, even as Bolan pitched him over his shoulder.

Gribov slammed onto his back and Bolan stomped on his throat, pinning him beneath the rising water. Gribov clawed at his leg with desperate strength, but like Drenk earlier, Bolan had the leverage and the weight to make his bid for freedom useless. And he had no intention of letting Gribov get up. With a twist of his shoulders, he dislocated Gribov's arm. Bubbles erupted from Gribov's mouth as he screamed. Then, as Bolan pressed down on his throat, his screams stopped. Bolan counted to ten and then let Gribov's arm flop uselessly into the water.

Bolan retrieved his pistol and checked it, ensuring that the water hadn't damaged it. As he did so, he heard a splash and spun. Gribov, face purple, mouth gaping, lurched toward him, good hand extended. Bolan fired once, twice and a third time, putting the last bullet right between Gribov's eyes. The big man toppled forward into the still rising water to join Drenk. Bolan released a breath he hadn't realized he'd been holding and lowered his pistol.

He saw Pierpoint's body and felt a moment of sadness. He'd only known the man for a little while, but he'd recognized a certain kinship. A strength of will, a determination that had resembled Bolan's own. Pierpoint had wanted to make the world a better place. And he'd died for it.

"Garrand," he said slowly. The mercenary had hightailed it when Drenk and Gribov had shown up.

There was only one place he could go. Ignoring the ache settling into his strained limbs, Bolan began to run. He had to catch Garrand.

The man couldn't be allowed to escape.

20

Bolan burst through the door and into the cove accompanied by a wave of seawater. It surged around him, tugging at him, trying to pull him off his feet as he moved toward the bobbing shapes of several speedboats and Jet Skis tied to a metal security bar. He could see at least half of the boats were missing, and Bolan felt a wash of relief. At least Carmichael and the others had gotten away. The pirates' speedboats were gone, as well. Maybe Axmed had made it off after all.

He caught sight of Garrand aboard one of the Jet Skis. The vehicle growled to life as he bent over the controls. Bolan took aim with the Desert Eagle and fired, but the water crashing against him threw off his shot. Garrand cursed and water bubbled up into foam as the Jet Ski began to move. Bolan made to fire again, but the Desert Eagle clicked empty. He holstered the weapon as he ran.

Garrand twisted around, his own weapon in his

hand, and for a moment Bolan thought he was going to shoot him. Instead, Garrand took aim at the cable that held his Jet Ski connected to the security bar and fired, snapping the cable in half.

Bolan lunged for the dangling end of the cable and his fingers closed around it even as the watercraft shot away, like a bullet from a gun. He was dragged behind it with pulverizing speed, his body coring through the water in a tunnel of froth. Garrand didn't look back. Bolan held tight to the cable; there was nothing else for it. If he let go, Garrand would escape. And the Executioner didn't intend to let that happen.

The Jet Ski wobbled beneath the weight of its burden as it thrummed across the water toward the distant coastline. Bolan gritted his teeth as the water pounded against him like innumerable blows, and he began to haul himself along the cable's squirming length as quickly as he could, hand over hand. Muscles burning, hands raw, he began to close the distance just as Garrand finally noticed him.

The mercenary glanced back, a snarl distorting his features. Bolan kept moving, his world narrowing to the back of the Jet Ski. Garrand pulled his pistol and thrust it beneath his arm, bracing it against his side in order to fire. He pulled the trigger again and again. Bullets punched through the water on either side of Bolan, narrowly missing him. He ignored them, ignored the urge to let go of the rope and get out of range, and kept hauling himself forward. Garrand emptied his clip, cursing loudly. A bullet tore through the sleeve of Bolan's fatigues as he finally reached the back of the Jet Ski.

His fingers dug into the hard rubber of the platform, and his shoulders screamed as he tore himself free of the water in an explosion of spray. The Jet Ski bucked as Bolan thrust himself up into a half crouch, one hand grabbing a handful of Garrand's shirt. Garrand twisted like a snake, his pistol extended. Bolan reacted instantly, catching the barrel between his hands. He wrenched it from Garrand's grasp and flung it away. Garrand kicked back at him, nearly dislodging the Executioner from his perch.

As Bolan fought to maintain his balance, Garrand drew the knife sheathed on his hip. "This is going to end now!" he roared, twisting around and stabbing at Bolan with the knife. Bolan ducked and the blade sawed over his shoulder, dragging pain in its wake. He slammed a fist into Garrand's side, his knuckles crashing against the man's ribs. Garrand drove an elbow back, catching Bolan in the eye. The Jet Ski growled as it crested a wave, nearly dislodging them both. Blood poured down Bolan's shoulder and arm, but he ignored the pain and kept hold of his opponent. He punched Garrand again, driving hammer-like blows into the mercenary's kidney and ribs.

Garrand hacked at him with the knife, catching his cheek and scalp with the tip of the blade. Bolan reached up and caught Garrand's wrist. He squeezed, trying to force the other man to drop the blade, but Garrand was stronger than he looked. They pulled against one another, each man trying to outmuscle the other. Then, the Jet Ski slewed wildly as it caught a wave wrong, and Bolan felt his feet leave the platform. Garrand cursed as they struck the water together and were bowled under by another wave.

Streamers of red spiraled around Bolan as he

fought for control of the knife. Garrand clawed for his eyes, and Bolan drove a blow into his nose. Despite the cloying grip of the water, bone crunched and crimson blossomed beneath his knuckles. Garrand floated back in a rush of bubbles, and Bolan snatched the knife from his grip. Out of the corner of his eye, he saw dark shapes circling.

The sharks came from all directions, jaws agape, drawn by Bolan's blood in the water. Normally, sharks didn't care for humans. But the scent of blood had driven them into a feeding frenzy. As a trap of triangular teeth closed in, the Executioner swept the knife out, slashing at the shark's snout. It veered off, trailing blood, and other sharks closed in on it. Bolan, lungs beginning to ache, spun in place, searching for Garrand, but he was too late. Hands closed around his throat, and a knee drove up into his sternum.

The Executioner gasped, losing what little air he'd instinctively sucked into his lungs before they'd gone under. He was knocked back through the choppy waters by the force of the blow, and his back struck something rough. The passage of a shark spun him in a slow circle, and acting on instinct he slashed its flank. It pivoted away and was soon lost in the terrible, silent cacophony of the feeding frenzy.

Bolan thrust himself toward the surface, still holding tight to the knife. He caught sight of Garrand swimming for the bobbing Jet Ski. Bolan dove after him with powerful strokes. He did his best to ignore the circling sharks and the weakness growing in his limbs as he concentrated on the mercenary's rapidly dwindling form. *You're not getting away from me,* he thought, but the truth was, Garrand had a head start, and he was closer to the Jet Ski. He was going to escape, and there was little the Executioner could do to stop him.

Not without a miracle, at any rate.

Even as the thought occurred to him, a shark hit Garrand like a cannonball. It came out of nowhere, so fast that Bolan hadn't noticed its approach and wouldn't have had time to react even if he had. Garrand's eyes bulged as he twisted about, his leg and hip caught in the shark's jaws, and a scream bubbled from his throat as he was ripped away, out of Bolan's reach, and carried into the darkness. More sharks joined the first, arrowing toward the mercenary's struggling form, drawn by the dark streams of blood rising like an infernal halo around him. Bolan turned away and swam for the surface.

He sucked in a lungful of air and looked around. The sea was heaving, and he saw black, darting shapes everywhere. Bolan felt a chill crawl along his spine. He still had Garrand's knife, but it wasn't going to do much against the flotilla of ravenous sharks. He'd suffer the same fate as Garrand if he were lucky. If not, it'd be a slower death as the sharks took pieces from him at their leisure.

Bolan sought out the shore. If he could make it close enough for the tide to carry him the rest of the way, he might have a chance. Ignoring the fatigue that sought to anchor his limbs and the ache pulsing in his head, he threw one arm over the over, pulling himself through the water toward the distant black line on the horizon.

But even as he swam, he knew he wasn't going to make it. He was running on fumes, and there were too many hungry predators between him and dry land. But he didn't stop, and he didn't slow his pace. He thought of all that he had accomplished and all that he still had left to do. There were more Claricuzios in the world, more Garrands and Gribovs—legions of them. The Executioner had spilled an ocean of blood, but there were oceans yet to be spilled if the world had any justice at all.

My work is not yet done. The thought hammered at his brain, driving back the clouds of fatigue, spurring him on. It was as close as he had ever come to a prayer. He wouldn't die here. He couldn't. Not in this sea, a victim of circumstance, lost and forgotten. This was not how he was fated to die. So he pushed himself on, past the limits of strength and into the red edges of exhaustion.

But the sharks followed. One, bolder than the others, or perhaps simply more curious, came at Bolan from the side. It struck him, knocking him through the water. He slashed at the creature as it circled him, driving it back, but not for long. The impact had sapped what little strength he had summoned. He felt hollow and wrung out. He followed the shark with his eyes as it drew closer and closer, tightening the metaphorical noose.

Bolan willed the shark to come closer, prepared to inflict as much damage as he could with the blade. "Come on," he said. The words came out sharp and hoarse. The shark plowed on, tearing through the water now as if in response to his challenge.

As the Executioner, knife in hand, prepared to sell his life dearly, a bullet plucked at the shark's triangular head. The animal veered off as more bullets followed. Whether it had been hit or not, Bolan couldn't say. Either way, it was leaving. He turned and saw a familiar smile beaming down at him.

"Still alive, then? Maybe I owe Spence an apology, huh?" Axmed said as he helped his men haul Bolan into the boat. "That was a dirty trick you pulled, locking us out of the cove. By rights, I should leave you to the sharks."

Bolan spat seawater out of his mouth and shook his head. Every muscle felt as if it were tied in knots. He was bleeding, and his hands were blistered and raw, but he was alive. "Why didn't you?"

"What—and seem ungrateful? No, no, my friend. I owe you a debt for delivering such riches into my hands," Axmed said, patting the sopping wet satchel that lay in the bottom of the boat. Bolan recognized it immediately—Pierpoint's ransom money. "Several million, I think, though I only glanced at it. A good deal of money, especially for a poor pirate such as myself. I think I may at last retire…somewhere inland, far from the sea." He winked. "Then, perhaps not, huh?"

Bolan smiled. Justice had been done…for now. Evil men had been punished and the lives of the innocent had been preserved.

In the end, that was all that mattered to the Executioner.

21

The Red Sea

"Salvage crews were out before the *Demeter*'s sail went below the water line," Hal Brognola said, examining the cigar he'd taken out of his mouth moments ago. He'd chewed it almost to the nub. Bolan wondered if the other man had been worried about him and felt a flicker of affection for the big Fed.

"Only half of them were locals," Brognola went on. They sat on the aft deck of a fishing boat, ostensibly privately owned but in truth belonging lock, stock and barrel to the CIA. Spence was nearby, lying on a beach chair, his shirt open and his torso bandaged.

"Will they find anything?" Bolan asked, scratching at his own bandages. After Axmed had pulled him out of the water, the pirate had deposited him on shore and then fled, money in hand. Not long after, Brognola had shown up, a wounded Spence in tow, along with a CIA escort. Now they were on deck, dressed in civvies and pretending to be heading for a vacation on the Red Sea Riviera. Bolan's wounds ached, but the stitches were holding and he knew he'd be more or less recovered by the time they reached port.

"They better," Spence said. "We're paying them enough." He grinned at the expression on Bolan's face. "What? You thought we were going to let everything sit on the bottom of the gulf for the fish to play with?" He gestured and winced. Unlike Bolan, he wasn't going to get a clean bill of health for some time. Despite the help Spence had given him, Bolan didn't feel too sorry for him.

"That was my impression, yes," Bolan said. He looked out over the water, admiring the sunrise. They were several hours away from the Gulf of Aden and making their way north, toward the port of Eilat in Israeli waters on the Gulf of Aqaba. Spence had promised him transportation to wherever he wanted to go, and Bolan had decided to keep his appointment in Sicily with what remained of the Claricuzio organization. Already, his mind was formulating a plan of attack. Brognola had offered him Stony Man's resources, and Bolan had accepted.

"Yeah, well, you were wrong," Spence said. "Pierpoint had a lot of good ideas. The man might be dead, but it'd be a shame to let everything he worked for die with him."

Bolan frowned. Pierpoint's death still weighed on his mind, though he knew it hadn't been his fault. And Garrand had paid for betraying Pierpoint with his life. He closed his eyes, thinking of the look on the mercenary's face as the sharks had dragged him down in a cyclone of red-stained water. *Not a pleasant way to go,* he thought. He looked at Brognola. "What about Garrand's men? Some of them survived."

Brognola stuffed his cigar into his mouth and leaned back in his deck chair. "Already got eyes on it, Cooper. If any of them so much as ping the radar, we'll bring them in."

"Small fry," Spence said dismissively. He rubbed his chest. "Speaking of which—what happened to Gribov and the others?"

Bolan smiled. "Taken care of." Gribov's death alone had made the trip worth it, though from what little he'd learned of Drenk, the latter could have given Gribov a run for his money as far as nastiness was concerned. He wasn't sure what had happened to Walid or Kravitz, but there'd been no sign of them on or off the boat. He wondered if Gribov and Drenk had decided to eliminate the competition. Or perhaps Garrand had killed them to cover his tracks. Either way, he suspected they were dead and on the bottom of the sea with the others. *And it couldn't have happened to a nicer pair.*

Spence laughed. "You were right, Hal…he is thorough."

Brognola met Bolan's gaze and saluted with his cigar.

"What about Pierpoint's people—the *Demeter*'s crew? What will happen to them?" Bolan asked, flexing his bandaged hand. It would have its strength back by the time he got to Sicily. He could re-equip in Messina and begin the slow process of hunting down the names he'd gotten from Claricuzio's papers. There were at least twenty of them, all hardened Cosa Nostra soldiers, but nothing he couldn't handle. In fact, he was looking forward to it.

"They'll be fine. Pierpoint Solutions will still function, even without its CEO. They all have generous severance packages to look forward to," Spence said. His grin slipped. "Pierpoint was a classy guy, all idiocy aside. He made sure his people would be taken care of."

Bolan grunted but said nothing. He looked at his hands with their old scars and bruised knuckles. Spence was still talking, but Brognola was watching him silently.

After a moment, the big Fed said, "I don't think we'll need you for a while, Matt. Maybe you should take some downtime. You took a pretty good beating…"

"Just because you don't need me, doesn't mean I don't have work to do," Bolan said, not looking at the other man. His fingers curled into fists. "And I haven't yet had a beating I couldn't walk away from." He looked up. Seabirds wheeled overhead, crying raucously to one another. The sun was up now, and the air smelled like salt.

"Maybe not. But we're not getting any younger. Especially me," Brognola said gruffly. Bolan shook his head, but Brognola persisted. "How much you got left in the tank, pal? Are you sure you don't want to take a vacation? Just a few days…"

Bolan hesitated, considering. Then he thought about Sicily. What was left of the late Domingo Claricuzio's human-trafficking operations still needed to be rolled up and put to the torch and their operators left in shallow graves. Innocent men and women

were suffering right now, a suffering he could allevi-
ate with a well-timed application of lead.

Wounded and tired as he was, the Executioner still
had a job to do. He looked at Brognola and smiled.

"Maybe one day," Bolan said, "but not today."

* * * * *

UPCOMING TITLES FROM

EXECUTIONER
DON PENDLETON'S

KILL SQUAD
Available March 2016
Nine million dollars goes missing from a Vegas casino, and an accountant threatens to spill to the Feds. But with the mob on his back, the moneyman skips town. Bolan must race across the country to secure the fugitive before the guy's bosses shut him up—forever.

DEATH GAME
Available June 2016
Two American scientists are kidnapped just as North Korea makes a play for Cold War–era ballistic missiles. Determined to save the scientists and prevent a world war, Bolan learns he's not the only one with his sights set on retrieving the missiles...

TERRORIST DISPATCH
Available September 2016
Atrocities continue in the Ukraine and the adjoining Crimean Peninsula, annexed by Russia in March 2014. With no end in sight, a plan is hatched to force American involvement by sending Ukrainian militants to strike Washington, DC, killing civilians and seizing the Lincoln Memorial as protest against their homeland's threat from Russia. Can Bolan bring the war home to the plotters' doorstep?

COMBAT MACHINES
Available December 2016
What began in a Romanian orphanage twenty years earlier, when a man walked away with ten children and disappeared, leads Mack Bolan and a team of Interpol agents to fend off a group of "invisible" assassins carving their way across Europe...toward the USA.

*E*THE DON PENDLETON'S*XECUTIONER*

Check out this sneak preview of
KILL SQUAD
by Don Pendleton!

"This is crazy," Sherman said.

His words were ignored as Bolan assessed their position. In the confines of the rail car, there was no chance they could conceal themselves. They were in the open, with armed men facing them. Once the shooters decided to push their way through, it would become a turkey shoot. If Bolan had been on his own, he might have considered resisting. But he had Sherman to consider, plus the burden of the other passengers. If he put up a fight, any retaliatory gunfire could overlap and cause injury to the innocent. That was something Bolan refused to allow.

He and Sherman were in line for the hostile fire. Bolan accepted that—with reservations where Sherman was concerned. The man was making an attempt to right wrongs, and he didn't deserve to become a victim himself.

The only way out was for Bolan and Sherman to remove themselves from the situation, which was easier to consider than to achieve. The soldier glanced at the window. The landscape slid by, an area of undulating terrain, wide and empty.

Another burst of autofire drove slugs against the connecting door. This time a couple of slugs broke through.

Bolan had already considered what he knew to be his

and Sherman's only option. He made his decision. He triggered a triburst through the connecting door to force the opposition back, even if it was only a brief distraction.

"Harry, let's go," he said. "Stay low and head for the other door."

"What...?"

"Do it, Harry, before those guys come our way."

Bolan fired off another triburst. Crouching, they made for the connecting door at the far end of the car. Bolan flung it open and hustled Sherman through. They paused on the swaying, open platform between the two cars, the rattle and rumble of the train loud in their ears.

The ground swept by, a spread of green below the slope that bordered the track.

Bolan glanced back through the connecting door and saw armed men moving into view. This time he held the Beretta in both hands and fired. Glass shattered. Bolan saw one man fall and the others pull aside. The delay would only last for seconds. He holstered the 93-R and zipped up his jacket.

"Have you ever jumped from a moving train?"

Don't miss
KILL SQUAD by Don Pendleton,
available March 2016 wherever
Gold Eagle® books and ebooks are sold.

GEXEXP446

STONY MAN®

"As the President's extralegal arm, Stony Man employs high-tech ordnance and weaponry to annihilate threats to the USA and to defenseless populations everywhere."

This larger format series, with a more high-tech focus than the other two Bolan series, features the ultracovert Stony Man Farm facility situated in the Blue Ridge Mountains of Virginia. It serves as the operations center for a team of dedicated cybernetic experts who provide mission control guidance and backup for the Able Team and Phoenix Force commandos, including ace pilot Jack Grimaldi, in the field.

Available wherever Gold Eagle® books and ebooks are sold.

GOLD EAGLE®

DON PENDLETON'S MACK BOLAN®

"Sanctioned by the Oval Office, Mack Bolan's mandate is to defuse threats against Americans and to protect the innocent and powerless anywhere in the world."

This longer format series features Mack Bolan and presents action/adventure storylines with an epic sweep that includes subplots. Bolan is supported by the Stony Man Farm teams, and can elicit assistance from allies that he encounters while on mission.

Available wherever Gold Eagle® books and ebooks are sold.

GOLD EAGLE®

JAMES AXLER
DEATHLANDS®

The saga that asks "What if a global nuclear war comes to pass?" and delivers gripping adventure and suspense in the grim postapocalyptic USA.

Set in the ruins of America one hundred years after a nuclear war devastated the world, a group of warrior survivalists, led by the intrepid Ryan Cawdor, search for a better future. In their struggle, the group is driven to persevere—even resorting to the secret devices created by the mistrusted "whitecoats" of prewar science.

Since the nukecaust, the American dream has been reduced to a daily fight for survival. In the hellish landscape of Deathlands, few dare to dream of a better tomorrow. But Ryan Cawdor and his companions press on, driven by the need for a future less treacherous than the present.

**Available wherever Gold Eagle®
books and ebooks are sold.**

GOLD EAGLE®